DIARY
of a Wimpy Kid

小屁孩日记 ⑰
——"砰、砰、砰"家庭旅行

[美] 杰夫·金尼 著

朱力安 译

胡子大叔

格雷

SPM

南方出版传媒

新世纪出版社

·广州·

本书简体中文版由美国Harry N. Abrams公司通过中国Creative Excellence Rights Agency独家授权

版权合同登记号：19-2014-178号

图书在版编目（CIP）数据

小屁孩日记⑰："砰、砰、砰"家庭旅行 /（美）杰夫·金尼著；朱力安译. —广州：新世纪出版社，2015.3（2016.6重印）

ISBN 978-7-5405-8774-1

Ⅰ.①小… Ⅱ.①杰… ②朱… Ⅲ.①漫画—作品集—美国—现代 Ⅳ.①J238.2

中国版本图书馆CIP数据核字（2014）第275515号

出 版 人：孙泽军
选题策划：林 铨 王小斌
责任编辑：傅 琨 廖晓威
责任技编：王建慧

小屁孩日记⑰ —— "砰、砰、砰"家庭旅行
XIAOPIHAI RIJI⑰ —— "PENG、PENG、PENG" JIATING LUXING
［美］杰夫·金尼 著 朱力安 译

出版发行：新世纪出版社
　　　　（广州市大沙头四马路10号 邮政编码：510102）
经 销：全国新华书店
印 刷：湛江南华印务有限公司
开 本：890mm × 1240mm 1/32
印 张：6.75 字 数：130千字
版 次：2015年3月第1版
印 次：2016年6月第5次印刷
定 价：18.50元

质量监督电话：020-83797655 购书咨询电话：020-83781545

"小屁孩之父"杰夫·金尼致中国粉丝

中国的"哈屁族":

你们好!

从小我就对中国很着迷,现在能给中国读者写信真是我的荣幸啊。我从来没想过自己会成为作家,更没想到我的作品会流传到你们的国家,一个离我家十万八千里的地方。

当我还是个小屁孩的时候,我和我的朋友曾试着挖地洞,希望一直挖下去就能到地球另一端的中国。不一会儿,我们就放弃了这个想法(要知道,挖洞是件多辛苦的事儿啊!);但现在通过我的这些作品,我终于到中国来了——只是通过另一种方式,跟我的想象有点不一样的方式。

谢谢你们让《小屁孩日记》在中国成为畅销书。我希望你们觉得这些故事是有趣的,也希望这些故事对你们是一种激励,让你们有朝一日也成为作家和漫画家。我是幸运的,因为我的梦想就是成为一个漫画家,而现在这个梦想实现了。不管你们的梦想是什么,我都希望你们梦想成真。

我希望有朝一日能亲身到中国看看。这是个将要实现的梦想!

希望你们喜欢《小屁孩日记》。再次感谢你们对这套书的喜爱!

 杰夫

A Letter to Chinese Readers

Hello to all my fans in China!

I've had a fascination with China ever since I was a boy, and it's a real privilege to be writing to you now. I never could have imagined that I would become an author, and that my work would reach a place as far from my home as your own country.

When I was a kid, my friends and I tried to dig a hole in the ground, because we hoped we could reach China on the other side of the earth. We gave up after a few minutes (digging is hard!), but with these books, I'm getting to reach your country... just in a different way than I had imagined.

*Thank you so much for making **Diary of a Wimpy Kid** a success in your country. I hope you find the stories funny and that they inspire you to become writers and cartoonists. I feel very fortunate to have achieved my dream to become a cartoonist, and I hope you achieve your dream, too... whatever it might be.*

I hope to one day visit China. It would be a dream come true!

*I hope you enjoy the **Wimpy Kid** books. Thank you again for embracing my books!*

Jeff

有趣的书，好玩的书

夏致

这是一个美国中学男生的日记。他为自己的瘦小个子而苦恼，老是会担心被同班的大块头欺负，会感慨"为什么分班不是按个头分而是按年龄分"。这是他心里一道小小的自卑，可是另一方面呢，他又为自己的脑瓜比别人灵光而沾沾自喜，心里嘲笑同班同学是笨蛋，老想投机取巧偷懒。

他在老妈的要求下写日记，幻想着自己成名后拿日记本应付蜂拥而至的记者；他特意在分班时装得不会念书，好让自己被分进基础班，打的主意是"尽可能降低别人对你的期望值，这样即使最后你可能几乎什么都不用干，也总能给他们带来惊喜"；他喜欢玩电子游戏，可是他爸爸常常把他赶出家去，好让他多活动一下。结果他跑到朋友家里去继续打游戏，然后在回家的路上用别人家的喷水器弄湿身子，扮成一身大汗的样子；他眼红自己的好朋友手受伤以后得到女生的百般呵护，就故意用绷带把自己的手掌缠得严严实实的装伤员，没招来女生的关注反惹来自己不想搭理的人；不过，一山还有一山高，格雷再聪明，在家里还是敌不过哥哥罗德里克，还是被耍得团团转；而正在上幼儿园的弟弟曼尼可以"恃小卖小"，无论怎么捣蛋都有爸妈护着，让格雷无可奈何。

这个狡黠、机趣、自恋、胆小、爱出风头、喜欢懒散的男孩，一点都不符合人们心目中的那种懂事上进的好孩子形象，奇怪的是这个缺点不少的男孩子让我忍不住喜欢他。

人们总想对生活中的一切事情贴上个"好"或"坏"的标签。要是找不出它的实在可见的好处，它就一定是"坏"，是没有价值的。

单纯的有趣，让我们增添几分好感和热爱，这难道不是比读书学习考试重要得多的事情吗？！生活就像一个蜜糖罐子，我们是趴在桌子边踮高脚尖伸出手，眼巴巴地瞅着罐子的孩子。有趣不就是蜂蜜的滋味吗？

翻开这本书后，我每次笑声与下一次笑声之间停顿不超过5分钟。一是因为格雷满脑子的鬼主意和诡辩，实在让人忍俊不禁。二是因为我还能毫不费劲地明白他的想法，一下子就捕捉到格雷的逻辑好笑在哪里，然后会心一笑。

小学二年级的时候我和同班的男生打架；初一的时候放学后我在黑板上写"某某某（男生）是个大笨蛋"；初二的时候，同桌的男生起立回答老师提问，我偷偷移开他的椅子，让他的屁股结结实实地亲吻了地面……我对初中男生的记忆少得可怜，到了高中，进了一所重点中学，大多数的男生要么是专心学习的乖男孩，要么是个性飞扬的早熟少年。除了愚人节和邻班的同学集体调换教室糊弄老师以外，男生们很少再玩恶作剧了。仿佛大家不约而同都知道，自己已经过了有资格耍小聪明，并且耍完以后别人会觉得自己可爱的年龄了。

如果你是一位超过中学年龄的大朋友，欢迎你和我在阅读时光中做一次短暂的童年之旅；如果你是格雷的同龄人，我真羡慕你们，因为你们读了这本日记之后，还可以在自己的周围发现比格雷的经历更妙趣横生的小故事，让阅读的美好体验延续到生活里。

要是给我一个机会再过一次童年，我一定会睁大自己还没有患上近视的眼睛，仔细发掘身边有趣的小事情，拿起笔记录下来。亲爱的读者，不知道当你读完这本小书后，是否也有同样的感觉？

片刻之后我转念一想，也许从现在开始，还来得及呢。作者创作这本图画日记那年是30岁，那么说来我还有9年时间呢。

一种简单的快乐

刘恺威

　　我接触《小屁孩日记》的时间其实并不长，是大约在一年多以前，我从香港飞回横店时，在机场的书店里看到了《小屁孩日记》的漫画。可能每一个人喜爱的漫画风格都不太一样，比如有人喜欢美式的、日系的、中国风的，有人注重写实感的，而我个人就比较偏向于这种线条简单的、随性的漫画，而且人物表情也都非常可爱。所以当时一下子就被封面吸引住了，再翻了翻内容，越看越觉得开心有趣，所以立刻就买下了它。

　　说实话，我并不认为《小屁孩日记》只是一本简单的儿童读物。我向别人推荐它的时候也会说，它是一本可以给大人看的漫画书，可以让整个人都感受到那种纯粹的开心。可能大家或多或少都会有这样的感受，当我们离开学校出来工作以后，渐渐地变得忙碌、和家人聚在一起的时间越来越少，也无法避免地接收到一些压力和负面情绪，对生活和社会的认知也变得更加复杂，有时候会感觉很累，心情烦躁，但如果真的自问为什么会这么累，究竟在辛苦追求着什么的时候，自己却又没有真正的答案……这并不是说我对成年后的生活有多么悲观，但像小孩子一样简单的快乐，确实离成年人越来越远了。但当我在看到《小屁孩日记》的时候，我却突然间想起了自己童年时那种纯真、简单的生活，这也是我决定买下这本漫画的原因之一。看《小屁孩日记》会让我把自己带回正轨，审核自己，检查一下自己最近的情绪、状况，还是要回到人的根本——开心。

　　我到现在也喜欢随手画一些小屁孩的画像来送给大家，这个也是最近一年来形成的习惯，因为自己大学读的是建筑，平时就喜欢随手画些东西，喜欢上小屁孩之后就开始画里面的人物，别看这个漫画线条简单，但想要用最简单的线条画出漫画里那种可爱的感觉，反而挺花功夫的。除了小屁孩这个主角之外，我最喜欢画的就是他的弟弟。弟弟是个特别爱搞鬼的小孩，而且长着一张让人特别想去捏他的脸。这兄弟俩的故事经常会让我想起我跟我妹妹的关系，我妹妹小时候也总是被我"欺负"，比如捏她的脸啊、整蛊她啊，但如果遇到了外人欺负妹妹，自己绝对是第一个站出来保护她的人。

六月

当了这么多年小·屁孩，要说学到什么的话，那就是人对自己的命运一点话事权都没有。

自从学校放假之后，我就没有什么非做不可的事儿，也没什么非去不可的地方了。只要空调还能出冷风，遥控器里有电池，我这个惬意的暑假就算是妥妥儿的了。

结果冷不防出了这事儿……

大家收拾好行李。我们要来一次自驾游！

老妈不打招呼就自作主张安排旅游，这已经不是第一次了。去年暑假第一天，她说我们要去北边那个州待几天，到疗养院看罗莱塔姨妈。

这可不是我想象中的美好暑假的开端……有一次我们去看罗莱塔姨妈，她的室友一把将我抱住，死活不放，直到有个护理员送她一个碎巧克力松饼才肯松手。

1

不过老妈只是吓吓我们而已。第二天吃早餐的时候，她才宣布我们真正要去的地方。

我们要去迪斯尼乐园！

哥哥罗德里克和我都很高兴，因为我们都担心暑假第一周要在疗养院玩沙狐球打发时间。

可是弟弟曼尼听说计划有变，完全无法接受。老妈把原定看望罗莱塔姨妈的这趟旅行吹上了天，结果曼尼真的满心期待。

　　最后我们为了去看罗莱塔姨妈，只好推迟迪斯尼之旅。一般人都以为，老妈吃过这次教训，应该不会再乱搞突击旅行了。

滑动

　　这次自驾游的点子出自哪里我是一清二楚，全都因为新一期《全家乐逍遥》杂志就在今天寄到的那堆新邮件里。

　　要我来猜的话，我们家90%的集体活动都是老妈从那本杂志里学来的。一看到最新那期，我就知道老妈又要蠢蠢欲动了。

我翻过几次《全家乐逍遥》，不得不承认，里面的彩图总能让一切都显得乐趣十足。

不过肯定是我们这家人有点小问题，因为我们的实际状况从来跟杂志上印的不一样。

不过我看老妈是永不言败的那种人。她说这次自驾游一定会很棒，一家人在车里共度时光也是一种"亲情交流"。

我试图劝她放过我们，让我们做点正常人做的事，比如找个水上乐园玩一天，但她不听。

她说这次旅游的精髓就在于不走寻常路，要"货真价实"地体验一把。

我以为老妈好歹事先跟老爸商量过，不过看来我是错了。因为老爸下班回家后，他的吃惊程度不亚于我们。

老爸说这不是个休假的好时机，而且不到万不得已他不想动用假期。不过老妈说，世上再没有比跟家人共度时光更重要的事了。

然后老爸说他真的很想这周末拖船下水。如果去自驾游，他就没法去开船了。

老爸跟老妈总体来说处得不错，不过有件事情一提起来，两人必定吵架，那就是老爸的那条船。

几年前的一天，老妈派老爸出门买牛奶，老爸在路上看到有人在自家院子里甩卖旧船。结果一眨眼的功夫，船就到了我们家的车道上。

老妈大发雷霆，埋怨老爸不跟她商量，因为船只保养很费工夫。

不过老爸说他一直梦想有一艘自己的船，这样我们全家每周末都能在海上度过。

于是老爸获准把船留下，他看上去开心极了。不过后来情况就急转直下了。

几天后，业主委员会来人敲了我们家的门。

他们说社区有规定，不允许把船停在房前，勒令老爸把船挪到后院。

再后来，因为老爸太忙，有船顾不上用，结果整个夏天船就在后院那么放着。入秋之后，老爸的一个同事跟他说，要给船做好御冬防寒措施。

老爸发现，给船做抗冻保养比他买船花的钱都多，于是决定赌一把。果不其然，两周之后，气温降到冰点以下，船身裂了条大缝。

开始下雪之后，老爸把船推到了后楼梯夹层下面。开春之后，老妈开始将房里的杂物往船上堆。

第二年夏天，老爸决定把船拿出来修一修。

可是当他要把船从楼梯夹层里拉出来的时候，他发现我们家的旧洗衣机里住进了一窝浣熊。

老爸打电话给除害公司，想请人来解决浣熊问题，可是当他了解了费用之后，还是决定亲自出马。

那个时候，曼尼已经听说有浣熊宝宝住在洗衣机里，老妈必须出面摆平这事了。

然后船就这么一直闲着。很久没听到楼梯夹层传来动物上窜下跳的声音了，所以我猜浣熊们已经搬走了。

老妈今天跟老爸说，夏天还长，剩下的日子里他尽可以带船下水，之后老爸就放弃争辩了。

老妈说一大早就出发，所以我们得开始收拾东西了。她只准大家拿"必需品"，这样家里的那辆小车才够放。

等我们把全部行李摆到车道上之后，谁都看得出车里搁不下。

　　老妈开始把所有东西过一遍，分出来两堆——一堆是必要的，一堆是不必要的。罗德里克很失落，因为他的好些"必需品"都被撤下了。

　　我有好些小·东西老妈不让带，真是岂有此理，曼尼的塑料马桶这么大，老妈都准带上车。

　　每次我们出门超过十五分钟，老妈就会带上曼尼的马桶"以防万一"。不过每次曼尼用马桶的时候我都浑身不自在。

　　老妈不准我和罗德里克带任何电子产品上路，虽然电子产品一点都不占地方。

　　她老说这年头孩子们不懂社交，因为他们就知道盯着电子屏幕。

　　不过我跟你说：等我有了孩子，他们想玩什么我就让他们玩什么。要我说，电子产品才是家庭幸福的关键。

　　即便老妈把车道上的每样东西都过了一遍，把不必要的东西全部剔除后，车里还是放不下所有东西。

　　我建议租一辆巨型房车，这样不仅有足够的空间放我们的东西，肯定还有多余的空间。

　　依我看，一家人要想和睦相处，每个人都得有自己的空间。有了那种高配置的房车，我们可以在路上连开几个星期，互相还不用打照面。

不过老妈说房车太贵，而且巨耗油，所以这个想法可以打住了。

罗德里克说我们可以弄一辆拖车在后面拖着，我觉得这个点子十分高明。

不过显然罗德里克是盘算着把拖车当成他的迷你公寓，所以这个主意也没戏了。

老爸插嘴，说了他自己的主意。他说空间不足的问题可以解决，只要把车里搁不下的东西放进船里，然后拖着船上路就好。

老妈意识到我们别无选择，所以就服软了。不过要把船拖到车道上，说来容易但做起来难。

不仅有各种杂物需要从船里搬出来，而且船底居然还长出一颗树来。我们花了三个小时才把船从楼梯夹层里折腾出来。顺带提一下，老妈并没有帮上多大忙。

把船拖上车道之后，老爸用封箱胶把船底的洞和船身的裂缝给补上了。

我只希望这次旅程这船千万别下水，最好连近水都免了。

因为据我所知，船上连救生工具都没有。

虽然加了条船，添了些空间，但小车里还是挤得满满当当的。我在最后一刻把枕头偷偷带上车，因为我觉得我好歹有权享有一件奢侈品。

我估计罗德里克想坐车后面，因为每次我们全家出行，他都想摊开四肢睡个觉。

我们时不时会忘记罗德里克还留在车里。

今年复活节，我们做礼拜都快做到一半，老妈才发现罗德里克根本没下车。

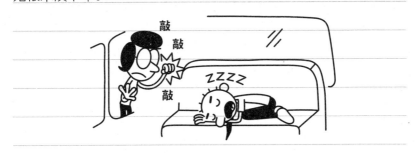

我们家以前还开旅行车的时候，我和罗德里克老是一起坐在后头面朝后窗的位置。有一次我们跟爸妈玩恶作剧，结果闯了大祸，警察把老爸跟老妈给拦了下来。

今天我们上车的时候，罗德里克主动把后座让给我。

我一口答应，不给他反悔的机会，但我早该知道，凡是他主动提议的，从来都没好事儿。

车还没有离开家门口的车道，老妈就说这次的旅行有一位"贵宾"加入。我还担心了一下，唯恐要再去接什么人上车，因为车里这么挤，那人恐怕只能坐车顶了。

不过老妈打开手提包，从里头取出一张彩绘小纸片。

取出

画的是扁平娃斯坦利，这是我上二年级时读过的一本书的主角。

　　斯坦利是个男生，有天晚上他卧室的布告板从墙上掉下来，把他给压扁了。

　　等大家把布告板掀起来的时候，他已经薄得就像一张纸了。

　　扁平娃可以把自己叠起来寄给奶奶，或者让哥哥拿他来放风筝。我觉得这样实在是酷毙了。

不过我跟你说，要是扁平娃有罗德里克这么个哥哥，我敢担保他连24小时都活不过。

我很喜欢那本书，但也被那本书吓到了。它害得我对布告板恐惧至极。

二年级的时候，老师让班上每个人给扁平娃填色然后剪下来，寄给远方的亲戚朋友。

收到的人要找个有趣的地方给扁平娃拍张照片，然后将扁平娃连同照片寄回。

我的死党罗利把扁平娃寄给了一堆亲戚，收到了大堆酷酷的照片。罗利还把它寄给了他远在亚洲的亲戚，那个人在中国长城上给扁平娃拍了张照片。

老妈寄送扁平娃的第一个对象就是她住在西雅图的表姐斯泰茜。但她是所托非人了。

斯泰茜是那种囤积成癖的人，连报纸杂志都不放过，老妈早该知道，将信寄给她表姐后，我的扁平娃是有去无回了。

往里塞

老妈今天说，但凡我们去到有意思的地方，她都会给新扁平娃拍张照，然后做成剪贴簿。我们一上高速公路，她就开始一通狂拍。不过我看她是太心急了，因为她拍的头几张都没什么保留价值。

老妈不拍照的时候，扁平娃就贴在前面空调的通风口上。我

21

只能说，它这一趟比我舒服多了。车的后窗开不了，气流都被行李箱堵住了，我这里一点冷气都没有。

让我更不自在的是，这次全程由老妈说了算。老妈总是想方设法给事情赋予教育意义，我就知道她要把这次旅途变成一堂大课。

从我小时候她就这样。我还记得有一次我被奶奶家的猫给抓伤了，老妈硬生生地要将情形扭转为"教育一刻"。

果不其然，今天车刚开了半小时，老妈就开始搬出教育那套了。

她从图书馆借来一堆西班牙语教学光盘，她说全家人要利用在路上的间隙学习一门外语。

老妈一直说，学外语是健脑的最佳方法。这或许有道理，不过我觉得她应该把真正的教学留给学校。

老妈认为让我早点接触外语是件好事，于是在我上一年级的时候，她就在早餐时间放西班牙语电视节目。

电视上说一句，老妈就学一句。不过她说出来的听着就感觉不大像。

结果最后我学了各种似是而非的表达。比如说，用西班牙语问别人的名字，应该说"Cómo te llamas"。好吧，我现在总算知道了，那是因为中学西班牙语课上教了。

不过我小时候，老妈跟我说"你叫什么名字"在西班牙语里面是"Te amo"，但其实"Te amo"的真正意思是"我爱你"。早知如此我就不会见人就说这句话了。

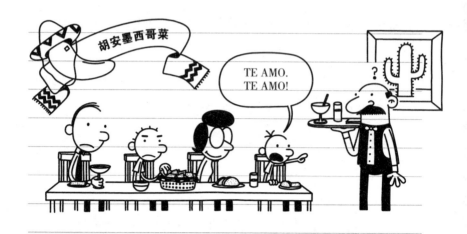

今天，老妈放完了前两张西班牙语光盘，不过她很崩溃，因为好像没人在听。于是她换了一招，说要玩一个她从杂志上读到的车上游戏。

这个游戏叫做"字母超市"，玩法是：第一个玩家要说一样以字母"A"打头的、能在超市里买到的东西。第二个人要说一样以"B"打头的东西，如此继续。

如果轮到谁说不出以指定字母打头的商品，这名玩家就出局了。

老妈让我先来，于是我说了"APPLE"（苹果），这是再明显不过的了。接下来是罗德里克，不过他说他实在想不出有什么食物以"B"打头。

我敢肯定他是为了退出游戏而故意撒谎，不过罗德里克这个人，没人能搞清楚他到底在想什么。

罗德里克出局后，就轮到曼尼了，他立刻就想到了。

老妈开始鼓掌，不过我严正指出，没有"BAPPLE"这个词。老妈说曼尼还在字母学习阶段，家人要以"鼓励"为主。

我退出游戏以示抗议。之后就只剩曼尼、老爸和老妈在玩了。我真心希望当初没把耳塞放进旅行包里，现在旅行包被压在一堆箱子下面拿不出来，因为接下来的一个半小时实在太难熬了。

他们一直在说吃的，搞得我都饿了。我看到下一个高速出口处有车上点餐的路标，于是问老妈能不能停下来买吃的。不过老妈说我们是不会在那种餐厅前停车的，因为他们没有"正经食物"。

她说快餐店用廉价塑料玩具来诱惑小·孩子吃高糖和高脂肪的东西，我们才不会上这种当。老妈说她早就准备好了比快餐不知好多少倍的东西，然后递给我一个写了我名字的午餐纸袋。

老妈说，"妈咪爱心餐"的创意来自《全家乐逍遥》，这我一点都不惊讶。

袋子里有一个吞拿鱼三明治、一个橙子和一小盒牛奶，外加被锡箔纸包住的一小团东西。

老妈说我必须先把水果吃掉才准打开锡箔纸，因为那是我的"奖品"。

真后悔当初没有立刻把锡箔纸打开。早知道奖品是一叠四则运算卡，我就不勉强吃下一整个橙子了。

罗德里克也在午餐袋里拿到了四则运算卡，我们都能预见事态会如何发展。所以赶在老妈把接下来半小时变成家教课之前，我抢先从老妈打包进大旅行包里面的游戏中取出一样。

我取出来的游戏叫"我坦白"，老妈看到之后兴奋得把四则运算卡的事儿全忘了。

我读了规则，相当简单：轮流从那叠卡片中取出一张读给周围的人听。

我坦白……

……我见过一个名人。

如果有玩家做过卡上写的事情，他们就能得1分。第一个拿够10分的玩家就赢了。

我刚开始还有点怀疑，不过不得不承认，这游戏玩下去其实还挺有意思的。我了解到好多以前不知道的关于老爸老妈的事。

原来老爸小时候养过一条变色龙当宠物，老妈曾经把头发染成金色，这都让我很吃惊。

信不信由你，连罗德里克都进入了游戏状态。他是唯一一个

为了排队买演唱会票而在外头露宿的，因此得了1分。另1分是因为他曾经让虫子进了耳朵，我对此记忆犹新。

老爸和罗德里克的比分僵持不下，都得了9分，谁能拿到下1分谁就能胜出。看到大家都很投入，玩得兴致勃勃，老妈好像很开心。

然后她抽出一张新卡片，念了题面。

我坦白，我曾经用卷筒纸对邻居房子进行恶作剧。

我确信老妈以为无人得分，已经直接伸手去摸下一张卡了。结果罗德里克突然像中了六合彩一样兴奋。

　　老妈认为罗德里克是为了得分而撒谎，不过他说这事儿千真万确。他说几个月前，邻居塔特尔太太报警说他们乐队排练噪音太大，于是他和队友就用卷筒纸给她的房子来了场恶作剧。

　　罗德里克还把整件事描述得绘声绘色，但老妈看上去一点都不觉得这事儿有趣。

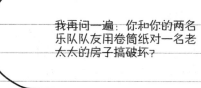

我再问一遍：你和你的两名乐队队友用卷筒纸对一名老太太的房子搞破坏？

如果是我，我就赶紧改口，说我是为了赢这一局而信口开河了。不过罗德里克没有抓住机会脱身。

不对，我们一共四个人。

老妈让老爸把车停在路边，然后把手机递给罗德里克，让他打电话跟塔特尔太太道歉，搞得车里的人都很尴尬。

对不起，我们用卷筒纸给您的房子搞破坏了……

……太太。

之后很长一段时间，车里一片死寂。老妈准备放下一张西班牙语光盘，幸好曼尼已经睡着了，她才没放。

你要是在曼尼小睡的时候吵醒他，他会大发雷霆，谁劝都不行。所以每次曼尼睡着的时候，老爸和老妈都千方百计让他保持沉睡状态。

我在曼尼那个年纪也特爱睡午觉。我以前每天午餐之后会睡一个小时。上小小班之后，我们有规定的午休时间，所有人都要铺毯子在地板上睡午觉。

要我说，小孩午休时间应该一直保持到大学毕业。不过我很快就了解到残酷的真相：小小班之后就没有午休时间了。

上幼儿园第一天，吃完零食之后，我问老师我们的毯子在哪儿，这样我们好躺下来"充一下电"。

不过她说幼儿园不设午休时段，我以为她在说笑。

哈哈，可不就是！

几分钟后，全班开始用纸袋子做玩偶。显然，我是唯一一个没有提前得到通知的人，因为班上其他人一天下来都没问题，只有我快撑不住了。

拖着
脚步

　　我很庆幸老妈记得带安抚奶嘴，因为只要曼尼嘴里叼着奶嘴，无论天翻地覆他都能继续睡。曼尼常用的奶嘴昨晚弄丢了，老爸跑去家附近的一家商店买了个新的，不过那是家卖搞怪道具的商店。

　　看上去怪怪的，不过跟普通的奶嘴一样好用。

当我们在收费站停下的时候，曼尼已经安详地睡了一个小时。老爸摇低车窗来买票，收费站的家伙嗓门巨大，听上去就像用扩音器在讲话。

曼尼开始躁动不安，奶嘴掉出来一半。幸好罗德里克眼疾手快，曼尼才能继续睡下去。

曼尼睡过去了，我猜老妈是有点郁闷的。她在地图上标了一堆地方，原本想下车观光的，现在只好直接开过去了。

曼尼的午休给我带来的问题是——我急需活动一下手脚，但没办法下车。

我尽量让自己舒服一点，但是周围都是东西，实在做不到。

幸好我的书包就在座位后面，伸手就能够到，里面有好些我的消遣读物和其他东西。

老妈总想让我读一些"充实自我"的书，但是书这方面，我知道自己的口味。自从上小学之后，我的最爱就是《内裤大盗》系列。

《内裤大盗》讲的是布赖斯和布罗迪两个男生穿越时空去偷

盗历史人物的内裤，然后拿回现代收藏到博物馆里。

我知道这听上去就很荒诞，但这个系列真的很好玩。

这套书在学校的男生里超级流行，不过老师对这套书恨之入骨，说它们"趣味低俗"。

五年级的时候，每次要交读书报告的时候，班里男生写的都是《内裤大盗》系列里的书。这使得我的老师特里太太对这个系列更加痛恨。

班上有个项目要求大家写信给自己喜爱的作者，当然，所有男生都选了米克·戴维斯。

不过特里太太非要我们选其他作者，我只好从图书馆随便抓了一本，然后给一个我闻所未闻的作者写了封信。

亲爱的霍桑先生：

老师让我们给作者写信，所以我就选了

你。我没读过你的任何作品（无意冒犯）。

我有几个问题想问你：

1. 你喜欢什么颜色？

2. 你喜欢什么动物？

3. 你喜欢什么口味的雪糕？

4. 你喜欢哪部超级英雄电影？

如能尽快回复，我将不胜感激，因为这项

作业是要计分的。

诚挚的，

格雷·赫夫利

不过我下笔写信之前是应该先查查书的出版年份的。

5月20日

亲爱的赫夫利先生：

很遗憾地告知您，您写信联系的作者霍桑

先生在一个世纪前就去世了。

有鉴于此，他无法对您的问题予以回复。

深表遗憾，

卡特里娜·韦尔克

出版方

家长也大多不喜欢《内裤大盗》系列。

说起来，家长教师联谊会那年还召开了一次大会，会议决定纳税人所付的钱不应用于图书馆购买《内裤大盗》之类的书。

放完春假后，我们回到学校，发现图书馆里的《内裤大盗》系列一本不剩。

这事直接造成的后果是——我们这一代的男生长大以后都不会阅读了，这下大人们该满意了吧。

学校把《内裤大盗》禁掉，却导致该系列比以前更火。有几个男生从家里把书偷带过来，然后跟别的男生交换。

有个男生还从日本走私回来一本《内裤大盗》日语版。我一个词都读不懂，不过光看图就可以知道是怎么回事儿了。

我还自发地给作者写了封信，告诉他我有多喜欢这个系列。

8月18日

亲爱的戴维斯先生：

我写信是为了告诉你，有人说你的书是垃圾，别听他们的，他们不懂。我认识的好些孩子（包括我自己）都觉得你的书非常棒。

我觉得内容很搞笑，我还想鼓励你多添加一些吃喝拉撒之类的内容。

诚挚的，

格雷·赫夫利

我还从来没有写过这种粉丝来信，我每天放学回家都会跑去信箱看看米克·戴维斯回信了没。

快一年之后，我终于收到了回信，我非常兴奋。

但我读到信之后，简直失望透了。

来自米克·戴维斯的信

亲爱的朋友：

很遗憾，由于粉丝来信数量过多，无法一一亲自回复。

不过我想跟你说的是，《内裤大盗24：林肯的秋裤》即将在各大书店有售，敬请关注！

米克·戴维斯

我倾注了这么多心血，得到的居然是一张广告，真是难以置信。

随手一扔

虽然这事儿有点倒胃口，但我还是喜欢他的书。

至少这个假期我还能想读什么就读什么。学校给罗德里克派了一整张必读书目的书单，好些书读起来似乎比较费劲。

简·爱

夏洛蒂·勃朗特

白鲸

赫尔曼·梅尔维尔

双城记

查尔斯·狄更斯

不过罗德里克可不是读书的人，所以他借来了书单上全部作品的电影版。

　　不过我觉得他的方法有点问题。他的暑期书单上有《魔戒》，不过他租电影的时候没仔细看标题。

　　罗德里克把电影看了两遍。看完第二遍之后，他跟老妈说，这书虽然不知道是谁写的，不过作者绝对是个天才。我猜当罗德里克的老师九月份读到他的读书报告时，肯定会无比困惑。

等我完成今天的阅读之后，当真需要下车走走了，不然我的双腿就要抽筋抽死了。

曼尼还在睡，不过他整个人颠倒过来了，不知道他是怎么做到的。

老妈注意到之后，就跟老爸说，今天就开到这儿吧，于是老爸从下一个出口下高速，然后把车停了下来。

我相当期待咱们能找个正经餐厅吃顿饭，不过老妈说预算有限，今晚要去超市买吃的带回去吃。

老爸在高速出口几英里之外找到了一家超市。不过老妈担心停车的话，曼尼会醒过来然后发飙。所以老妈给罗德里克写了一张购物单，把钱给了他。老爸在超市入口处把车开得超慢，方便罗德里克跳下车。

　　老爸在停车场绕了大概十圈。这可并不容易，要知道我们还拖着一条船呢。最后，罗德里克拿着两袋东西出来了。看上去他好像还给自己藏了点私货。

　　老爸给车掉了个头，罗德里克跳上车。然后我们就开始找地方过夜了，不过这个地区可以选的酒店都不大理想。

好些汽车旅店挂着大大的广告牌，上面写着"彩电"，依我看，今时今日这已经不值得夸口了吧。

老爸最后在一家有空调和游泳池的旅店前面把车停下。空调和游泳池听上去真不错，尤其是我白天已经热得不行了，坐在后座上光出汗就减掉了5磅。

我没有住过太多旅店，所以不好评价。不过要我猜的话，我们选的这家估计属于低端的。

大堂有股霉味儿，地毯上全是诡异的污渍。

不过大家都太累了，不想回车里重新找地方了。

我们拿到了房钥匙，走进房间发现里面一股烟味儿。被子和枕头上布满小洞，我确信这些是烟头烧出来的。

老爸从地上捡起一条毛巾又立刻丢掉，因为毛巾是湿的。

老妈回到前台，要求换房。不过接待员说旅店已满，我们拿到的是最后一间。

老妈说，如果是这样，我们要退房另找一家。不过接待员说旅店有规定，取消入住需要提前24小时，所以不给我们退钱。

老妈回房后跟大家说，虽然环境恶劣但我们要尽量改善。她跟老爸一起把被单床罩统统扯了下来。

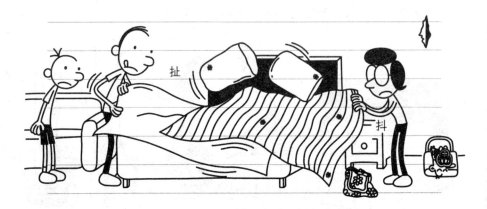

信不信由你，曼尼居然全程都睡过去了。老妈说，如果他这会儿醒过来，肯定会整夜都醒着，所以她要让他一直睡到早上。

老妈把曼尼搁在沙发床的中央，然后给他盖上一条毯子。

我们几个都饿坏了，于是把罗德里克买的食品倒出来。结果他压根没按老妈的购物单来买东西。

50

　　罗德里克本来应该买做三明治的材料、橙汁一类的东西，结果他只买了一堆他自己喜欢的。

　　该买的一样都没买，老妈很生气，不过罗德里克的借口是他看不懂老妈的笔迹。老妈说，居然买肉桂面包卷和速冻披萨饼，真是脑子不好使，这些东西需要烤箱，我们这里又没烤箱。

　　不过罗德里克说我们可以用微波炉加热。于是他把披萨饼放进微波炉里，要证明他的办法可行。

　　罗德里克以为那是个微波炉。其实是个保险柜。等他发现的时候，披萨饼已经锁在里头了。

　　老妈把剩下的零钱交给我，让我去楼下自动售货机，挑最有营养的东西来买。

　　于是我们自驾游第一晚吃了威化饼和薄荷糖当晚餐。

星期天

昨晚我们没法在房里看电视，也做不成别的，因为曼尼在沙发床上睡觉。

老妈连灯都不让开，于是我们就在黑暗中坐了一会儿，后来我和罗德里克决定去游泳池打发一下时间。

好吧，旅店门前的标志写着有游泳池，但没说游泳池里面没水。

而且看上去好像上次放水已经是五年前的事了。

游泳池旁边的一个热水浴缸倒是有水，不过另一家人在用。所以我和罗德里克就等着。

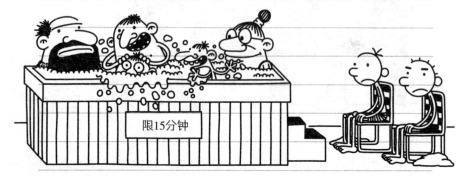

限15分钟

不幸的是，这家人很不识趣，不知道我们想泡热水澡，最后我和罗德里克只得又回了房间。

灯还是关着，老爸和老妈已经躺在床垫上睡着了。我猜他们肯定是累坏了，因为他们连外衣都没脱。

老爸和老妈睡了床，曼尼睡了沙发，我和罗德里克就没剩什么好的选择了。

我们去壁柜里找铁架床或充气床，但什么都没找到。

不过罗德里克还是快我一步。他把沙发靠垫收起来，在地上给自己铺了张床。5秒钟后，他就睡着了。

我看我干脆睡壁柜里好了，于是我从浴室找来毛巾铺在地上。

躺了一会儿，我闻到有股异味，我猜肯定是有老鼠死在通风管道里了。

我试着用毛巾捂住鼻子，但臭味反而更强烈了。

在这种环境下要睡着已经够难了，居然房里还有人开始打起呼噜来。幸好，我有对策。老爸和老妈都打呼噜，所以我早有准备，上路前带了耳塞。

不过房里太黑，我只在旅行包里找到一只耳塞，所以我只好给左耳塞上耳塞，把右耳贴着地。

我睡着了几分钟，但被门外的骚动吵醒了。

我从猫眼洞往外看，看到有东西呼啸而过，但我看不出是什么东西。于是我把门开了一道缝，想看看到底怎么回事儿。

原来是热水浴缸里那帮小孩在玩清洁车，把车往墙上撞。

难以置信，这些小孩的家长居然任由他们在半夜撒野，于是我走出去把他们教育了一番。

最小的那个孩子哭了起来，然后跑进房里，我一点都不觉得有什么不妥。可是一分钟后，门又开了，这次是他爹出来了。

我可不打算被一个只穿了内裤的成年人修理，于是我跑回房间把门锁上。然后我尽全力祈祷，希望门上的链条够结实，能把他挡在门外。

　　我猜那小·孩他爹是没看清我进了哪个门，因为他敲了别家的门。他狂敲了我们隔壁房的门，然后才放弃，回到自己房里。

　　险情过去之后，我在门把上挂了个牌子，以免那家伙又找回来。

一番折腾之后要再睡着可真困难，因为每次听到门外有人走过，我都大气不敢喘。

不知不觉，太阳就升起来了，曼尼也起床了。老妈打开电视，曼尼每次看电视都会跟电视说话。

曼尼喋喋不休让我有点心烦，不过我也没什么可抱怨的。我小时候跟他一模一样。

有一次我在看我喜欢的节目，主持人问了一个问题。

我只是随口一说，但电视里那家伙居然接我话了。

要是没出这事儿就好了。因为从那件事之后，很久以来我都以为电视里的人可以听到我说话。

其实，在我6岁生日的时候，老妈还一本正经地要我学会区分"想象中"的朋友和"现实中"的朋友。

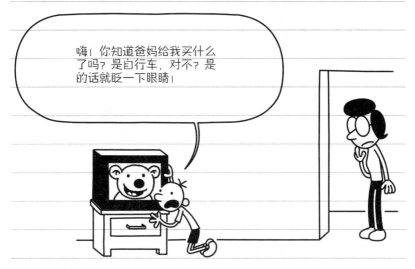

曼尼早上一开始跟他喜欢的电视人物对话，我就知道自己再也没法努力继续睡下去了。于是我干脆起床了。

起床之后，我找到了那股恶臭的来源。罗德里克把他的鞋子放进壁柜里了，而我整个晚上都在闻他的鞋味儿。

更悲剧的是，我用来捂住鼻子的"毛巾"原来是罗德里克的一只袜子。

　　说到罗德里克，曼尼跟电视的对话居然一点都没妨碍到他，他就在噪音中照睡不误。

你懂不懂蛙跳?

跳! 跳!

　　老爸早上等大家出门等得有点焦躁不安。平时他天一亮就起床，以便能早点到办公室，晚起晚出门这一套对他来说是行不通的。

　　终于，老妈把罗德里克弄起床，让他洗了个澡。我们到旅店附近的一个餐厅吃了早餐，然后回到车里。

　　老妈说，从现在开始，大家要作息一致，免得在路上浪费时间。不过她话还没说完，曼尼就在车座上又睡过去了。

　　老妈今天的大计是让我们去一个她在《全家乐逍遥》上读到过的乡村博览会。

　　我从来没参加过这种活动，不过看上去似乎值得一试。

还要好几个小·时才能开到博览会，也就是说我又要被塞进后座了，我已经开始觉得腻烦。谢天谢地，一小·时后，老妈提出跟我换位置。

我换到前座之后，感觉这里宽敞得令人难以置信。

不光是地方宽敞让人舒畅，我还有自己的温度控制旋钮和自己的杯托。

我想换个电台节目来听，不过老爸不让。他说听什么音乐由司机说了算。我觉得不公平，但我不打算抱怨，以免有被换回后座的风险。

老爸挑的音乐真烂，不过眼前的美景算是一种补偿吧。

坐在后头的时候，人对前面有什么完全没概念。坐在前面，我有了全新的感受，我几乎可以理解老妈为什么对这次自驾游充满热情了。

下了高速前往乡村博览会，我们在红灯前面停下来。前面是一辆小车，跟我们家的车型号完全相同，不过是紫色的。

车里的小孩看上去有点脸熟。一秒钟之后，我认出他们就是昨晚那群小孩。

我没告诉老爸和老妈那帮小孩和清洁车的事件，因为我担心这会影响我的高大形象。我跟胡子大叔遭遇的那段更加不必告诉他们。

紫色车里的孩子们立刻认出了我，开始朝我做各种鬼脸。

我才不会任这帮小混蛋欺负，所以我也朝他们做鬼脸。

那个瘦子做同样的鬼脸回敬给我，不过就在那一刻，红灯转绿，司机踩油加速。他们的小车往前一冲，那小孩整张脸就印在了车后窗上。

老爸从左侧超车，胡子大叔跟我结结实实打了个照面。

嗖

幸好不到几百米就到博览会的停车场了。停车之后，我打算在车里面等着，直到确定没被那辆紫色车跟踪才下来。

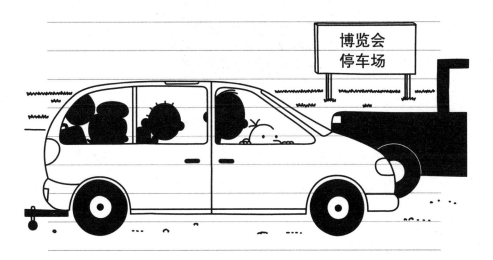

博览会
停车场

看上去我们已经脱险了。曼尼还在他的安全座椅上睡觉，所以老妈说她留在车里陪他，让其他人先进去。

博览会跟我想象中的大不相同。我以为里面有摩天轮和旋转木马之类的，不过看到的是关着牲口的帐篷和摆着当地美食的展位。

反正也饿了，于是我们直接开始找吃的。

有卖玉米热狗和炸甜甜圈的，一般大型博览会能见到的食品，这儿都有。不过这儿还有好些诡异的东西，比如炸牛油串。

老妈留在车里我还有点高兴，因为我很肯定这类食物按照她的定义是算不上"正经食物"的。

　　在露天市场走了一个小时后，老爸要回车里看看曼尼醒了没，他让我和罗德里克自己逛。

　　我们俩在里头转悠了好一会儿，直到我们发现有个帐篷，里面似乎在搞什么大型活动。

　　原来是终极恶臭鞋具大赛，谁的鞋子气味最恶劣就能拿到奖品。

　　帐篷前面很多人在排队，都是来提交参赛作品的。

终极恶臭
鞋具大赛

我让罗德里克参赛，因如果有人能获此殊荣，那个人非他莫属。

排队等候的时候，我跟罗德里克关于奖品归谁的问题争执起来。我说我们应该对半分，因为这是我的主意。不过他说他应该独得，因为这是他的鞋子，而且鞋子这么臭是他的功劳。

就在我们走到裁判桌之前，我们达成共识，作为罗德里克的代理人，我分得奖品的10%。

有些其他人的鞋子看上去状况比罗德里克的还要糟糕，我信心有点开始动摇。不过当裁判开始气味测评环节之后，胜负就见分晓了。

罗德里克赢得头奖，原来奖品是炸牛油串兑换券一张。我跟罗德里克说，这个全归他了，因为一想到再吃牛油我就有点作呕。

罗德里克问评委把鞋子要回来，不过他们说鞋子要留着参加全国大赛。所以罗德里克只能穿着一只鞋子四处走。我决定趁罗德里克慢慢吃他的炸牛油串的时候去周围的摊档看看。

这时险情出现了，我转了个弯，差点撞上胡子大叔全家。幸好我及时俯身躲了起来。

　　得知胡子大叔一家也在露天市场，我赶紧离开。

　　我去找罗德里克，但他肯定是先回车里了。于是我决定自己回去，不过半路经过一个关着牲口的帐篷，我在人群中看到了老妈的半截脑袋。

　　大家摩肩接踵，我努力穿过人群挤到老妈所在的位置。

　　正当我走到半路的时候，群众爆发出一阵欢呼。

好哇！

终于走到前面之后，我惊奇地发现曼尼站在人群之中，手里举着一张纸。

看来这似乎是一个比赛，猜一头猪的体重，看看谁能猜得最接近。曼尼猜得刚好分毫不差。

猜对的奖品是一头活生生的小猪宝宝。

老妈解释说他们只是来玩玩而已，并不真想要那头小猪。

不过大家似乎觉得蒙羞受辱，不接受老妈说"不"。

　　群情激愤，我很担心胡子大叔一家会过来牲口帐篷这边看热闹。幸好这时候老妈自己也想走了，于是我们就往出口处走去。

　　老爸坐在车里，把空调开得很大。看到老妈抱着一头猪回来，他被吓了一跳。

　　老妈跟老爸讲了曼尼比赛获胜赢得小·猪的全过程，不过老爸对此并不兴奋。

　　老爸说这头猪我们没法留，必须立刻送回博览会。

　　不过老妈说为时已晚，因为那头猪跟曼尼已经"心心相印"了。

　　老爸还是反对。他说猪是牲口，身上可能携带各种寄生虫。不过老妈说很多人都养猪作为宠物，还说她听过猪跟狗一样聪明。

　　然后罗德里克加入对话。他对保留小·猪投赞成票，他说这样一来我们每天早上就有免费培根可以吃了，就像养鸡取蛋一样。

　　要么是他不懂猪肉是怎么来的，要么就是他没把事情想明白。

　　我完全支持留住小·猪，只要能赶紧上路就好。

　　我看到跟我们的车相距几个车位的地方停了一辆紫色车，我很担心胡子大叔一家随时出现。

　　老爸终于服软了。他说如果要留猪，那猪只能待在船里。不过老妈说把猪搁在船里太"不人道"了，我们要在车里给它挪个地方。

问题是，车里确实没地方搁下它。不能让它满车乱跑，但也没法给它系上安全带。于是老妈把冷藏箱清空，然后把小猪放了进去。

一切处理好之后，我们终于从停车场出发了。

从停车场开出好几英里之后，我才终于舒了口气。

不过那头猪立刻开始捣乱了。我们一上高速，它就把冷藏箱弄翻了，然后开始用鼻子去拱老妈爱心餐的纸袋。

嗅嗅
哼哼
拱拱

我只好用力把猪扭回冷藏箱里，这次我用安全带箍住箱子，这样箱子就不会翻过来了。

老妈猜小猪饿了，所以她说我们得停车给它找点儿吃的。她的想法是我们去找个餐厅，然后打包点剩饭给它。这听上去太棒了，因为这就表示我们可以坐下来好好吃顿饭了。

我们在几英里外找到了一家吃饭的地方，老妈留在车里看着小·猪，我们几个进去吃。不过服务员看到罗德里克只穿了一只鞋子，谢绝他入内。

老爸让我和罗德里克轮流穿我的鞋进去吃。不过我真后悔让他先进去，因为他是世界上吃饭最慢的人。

回到车里，我们把剩下的玉米和蔬菜给了小·猪，它对着塑料餐盒就直接开吃了。

老妈开始用导航找地方过夜。她让罗德里克打电话问一家旅馆有没有空房。空房是有的，不过罗德里克口无遮拦，把事情搞糟了。

他们说，"不能带猪"。

老妈找到另一家几英里之外的旅馆，这次她自己来说。

旅馆就在收费站后面。距离出口不到几百米，车辆开始以龟速前进。

这对我可是个问题，因为我在餐厅喝了两大杯柠檬水，急需上洗手间。

我看到前面有个加油站，于是问老爸老妈我能不能跳下车，出去上洗手间，完事儿后再追上他们。

老爸不大赞成，因为他担心等我回来，车可能已经开过收费站了。不过这会儿显然小猪也想上洗手间，因为它正在冷藏箱里不停转着小圈。

老妈答应让我去加油站的卫生间，前提是我要带上小猪一起。

于是我用胳膊夹着它，横跨三条车道往加油站跑去。

　　我拧了一下男厕的把手，门上锁了。我一直等里面的人完事儿出来，但里面的人似乎一点都不着急。

　　我当时什么都不管了，我连女厕的把手也试过了，但同样是上了锁的。

　　我跑回车里——车才前进了1.5米左右。

　　我跟老妈说男女厕都有人，她说加油站的洗手间全天都上锁，我需要问店员拿钥匙。

　　于是我跑回加油站，跟前台说我急需用洗手间。

我对加油站的洗手间本来也说不上有什么期待，不过真实状况比我所能想象的要糟糕得多。

上厕所的时候有只牲口看着我，还真不习惯。但小·猪比我还尴尬，因为轮到它的时候，它一点都尿不出来。

我把钥匙还给店员后，发现我们的车正要穿过收费站。于是我快步穿过车流，刚好赶上。

可是在打开车门前，我本该注意到的——这辆车后面没有拖船。

我们家的车其实还在几辆车之后，等我上车的时候，小·猪看上去已经憋不住了。

我看老妈说猪很聪明还是有一定道理的，因为我一把它放到曼尼的马桶上，它立刻就会意了。

致谢

感谢我的好家人，感谢你们始终如一的关爱、支持和鼓励。

感谢阿布拉姆斯出版集团的所有人，感谢你们把每一本《小屁孩日记》都当成第一本来认真对待。尤其感谢查理·科赫曼、迈克尔·雅各布、詹森·威尔斯、韦罗妮卡·沃瑟曼、史蒂夫·塔格尔、苏珊·范米特、珍·格雷厄姆、查德·贝克尔曼、艾利森·热尔韦、埃莉萨·加西亚、埃丽卡·拉萨拉和斯科特·奥尔巴赫。

感谢我的所有国际出版商，是你们把格雷的故事带给了世界各地的孩子们。对过去跟大家结下的友谊，我深深感激。

感谢莎琳·热尔曼和安娜·塞萨里，感谢你们的所做的一切努力让事情件件有条不紊。

感谢保罗·森诺特和艾克·威廉斯，感谢你们的奇计妙策。

感谢好莱坞为把格雷·赫夫利搬上大大小小的荧幕而做出努力的所有人。尤其感谢西尔维·拉比诺、基思·弗里尔、妮娜·雅各布森、布拉德·辛普森、拉尔夫·米列罗、罗兰·波因德克斯特、伊丽莎白·加布勒和瓦妮莎·莫里森。

感谢Poptropica网站全体同仁，尤其感谢杰斯·布莱利尔。

作者简介

　　杰夫·金尼是《纽约时报》排行榜第一畅销书作者，四次荣获尼克国际儿童频道儿童之选最佳图书奖。杰夫被《时代》周刊评为"全球最具影响力100人"之一。杰夫也是Poptropica网站的创始人，该网站被《时代》周刊评为50佳网站之一。杰夫童年在华盛顿哥伦比亚特区度过，1995年移居新英格兰州。杰夫现与妻子和他的两个儿子居住在南马萨诸塞州，他正在筹办一家书店。

TO PRANAV

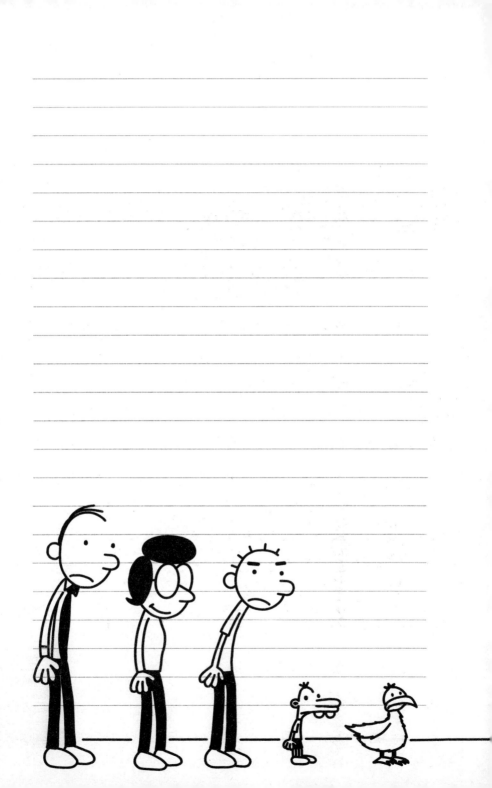

DIARY
of a
Wimpy Kid

by Jeff Kinney

JUNE

<u>Friday</u>

If there's one thing I've learned from my years of being a kid, it's that you have ZERO control over your own life.

Ever since school let out, I haven't had anything I've needed to DO or anywhere I've needed to BE. As long as the air-conditioning was working and the TV remote had batteries in it, I was all set for a relaxing summer vacation.

But then, out of the blue, THIS happened—

This isn't the FIRST time Mom has sprung a trip on us without any warning. Last year on the first day of summer, she said we were going upstate for a few days to visit Aunt Loretta at the nursing home.

It wasn't exactly my idea of a fun way to kick off the summer. One time when we visited Aunt Loretta, her roommate grabbed me and wouldn't let go until a staffer gave her a chocolate chip muffin.

But Mom was just bluffing about going to the nursing home. At breakfast the next morning, she told us where we were REALLY going.

Me and my brother Rodrick were happy, because we were both dreading spending the first week of summer vacation playing shuffleboard at a nursing home.

But when my little brother, Manny, heard about the change in plans, he totally LOST it. Mom had talked up the Aunt Loretta trip so much that Manny was actually EXCITED about going.

We ended up POSTPONING our trip to Disney so we could visit Aunt Loretta. You'd think Mom would've learned her lesson about surprise trips after THAT one.

SLIDE

I know EXACTLY where this road trip idea came from, because the new issue of "Family Frolic" magazine came in the mail today.

If I had to guess, I'd say 90% of everything we do as a family comes from ideas Mom gets from that magazine. And when I saw the latest issue, I knew it was gonna get Mom's wheels turning.

I've flipped through "Family Frolic" a few times, and I have to admit, the pictures always make everything look like a lot of fun.

But there must be something wrong with OUR family, because we can never measure up to the ones they show in the magazine.

I guess Mom's not giving up, though. She said this road trip is gonna be awesome and that spending a lot of time together in the car will be a "bonding" experience for the whole family.

I tried to talk her into letting us do something NORMAL, like going to a water park for the day, but Mom didn't want to hear it.

She said the whole point of this trip is to do things we've never done before and to have "authentic" experiences.

I thought Mom would've looped Dad in about her road trip idea, but apparently I was wrong. Because when he got home from work, he seemed just as surprised as us kids.

Dad told Mom it was a bad time to be away from work and he didn't want to use his vacation days unless he absolutely HAD to. But Mom said there's nothing more important than spending time with your family.

Then Dad told Mom he was really hoping to get his BOAT out on the water this weekend, and if we went on a road trip, he wouldn't be able to.

Mom and Dad get along pretty well in general, but the one thing that's guaranteed to cause a fight between them is Dad's boat.

A few years ago, Mom sent Dad out to get some milk, but along the way he spotted a boat for sale in someone's front yard. And before you knew it, the boat was in our driveway.

Mom was mad that Dad didn't check with her first, because having a boat is a ton of work.

But Dad said it was always his dream to own a
boat and that we could spend every weekend out
on the water as a family.

So Dad got to KEEP the boat, and he seemed
really happy. But things went downhill fast.

A few days later, some people from the
Homeowners' Association knocked on our door.

They said there were rules in our neighborhood against having a boat parked in front of your house and told Dad he had to move it to the back.

The boat sat in the backyard for the whole summer because Dad was too busy and didn't have time to use it. Then, in the fall, one of Dad's coworkers told him he'd have to WINTERIZE the boat to protect it from the cold weather.

Dad found out it would cost more to winterize the boat than it cost him to BUY it, so he decided he'd take his chances. And sure enough, two weeks later, when the temperature dropped below freezing, a big crack appeared in the hull.

When it started to snow, Dad rolled the boat
under the back deck, and it sat there all winter.
In the spring, Mom started using it to store all
sorts of junk from the house.

The next summer, Dad decided he was gonna fix
the boat.

But when he went to pull it out from under the deck, he discovered a family of raccoons living in our old washing machine.

Dad called an exterminator to get rid of the raccoons, but when he heard how much THAT was gonna cost, he decided to take care of it himself.

By then Manny had heard about the baby raccoons living in the washing machine, and Mom had to step in.

The boat's been sitting there ever since. I haven't heard any scurrying sounds coming from under the deck for a while, so I'm guessing the raccoons moved out.

Today, Mom told Dad he had the whole rest of the summer to get his boat out on the water, and he pretty much gave up after that.

Mom said we were gonna leave first thing in the morning, so we needed to start packing for the trip. She told everyone to bring the "bare essentials" so we could fit everything in the minivan.

But by the time we got all our stuff out in the driveway, it was pretty clear we had a space problem.

Mom started going through everything and sorting it into two piles—the things we needed and the things we didn't. Rodrick was pretty disappointed when some of his "essentials" didn't make the cut.

Mom made me leave a bunch of small stuff behind, which seemed pretty ridiculous considering that Manny's plastic potty was coming along for the ride.

Whenever we take a trip that's longer than fifteen minutes, Mom brings Manny's potty "just in case." But I get really uncomfortable whenever Manny uses it.

Mom wouldn't let me and Rodrick take any electronics on the trip, even though they barely take up any space.

She's always saying kids these days don't know how to socialize because they've constantly got their noses two inches from a screen.

But I'll tell you this: When I have kids, I'm gonna let them play with whatever kind of gadget they WANT. If you ask me, electronics are the key to family happiness.

Even after Mom went through every single item in the driveway and cut out all the things we didn't need, there was STILL way too much to fit in the van.

I suggested we rent one of those giant recreational vehicles, because we could fit all our stuff in it and have room to spare.

The way I see it, if you want the whole family to get along, everyone needs their own space. And with one of those souped-up RVs, we could spend WEEKS on the road without even bumping into one another.

But Mom said RVs are too expensive and they get terrible gas mileage, so that put an end to that idea.

Rodrick said maybe we could get one of those trailers you tow BEHIND the car, which sounded smart to me.

But it was pretty clear Rodrick was imagining the trailer as a sort of mini-apartment for HIMSELF, so that wasn't gonna fly, either.

Then Dad rang in with his OWN idea. He said we could solve the whole space issue by just putting the stuff that didn't fit in the van into the BOAT, which we could tow behind us.

I think Mom realized there wasn't really another option, so she caved in. But getting the boat into the driveway was easier said than done.

Not only did we have to take all the junk out of the boat, but it turned out there was a TREE growing through the bottom. It took three hours to get the boat out from under the deck, and let me just say Mom did not exactly go out of her way to help.

After we got the boat into the driveway, Dad patched up the hole in the bottom and the crack in the hull with some duct tape.

I just hope we're not going anywhere near water on this trip, though.

Because as far as I know, the boat didn't come
with any life preservers.

Saturday
Even with the added space we got from the boat,
the minivan was still pretty full. I snuck my pillow
on board at the last second, because I decided I
was entitled to at least ONE luxury item.

I figured Rodrick would want to sit in the back
of the van, because whenever we go anywhere as a
family, he likes to stretch out and take a nap.

Every once in a while we'll forget Rodrick is even
back there.

This Easter, we made it halfway through church before Mom realized Rodrick never made it out of the van.

Back when we had a station wagon, me and Rodrick used to sit in the way back TOGETHER, in a seat that faced the rear window. But we got in big trouble when we played a practical joke on Mom and Dad that ended up getting us pulled over by the police.

When we got in the van today, Rodrick offered me the backseat.

I accepted before he could change his mind, but I should've known his offer was too good to be true.

Before we pulled out of the driveway, Mom said we were taking a "special guest" along for the ride. For a second I was worried we were picking someone ELSE up, because with all our stuff in the van they'd have to sit on the ROOF.

But Mom opened her purse and pulled out a piece of paper with a drawing on it.

The drawing was Flat Stanley, a character from a book I read in second grade.

Flat Stanley is a boy who gets squashed by a bulletin board that falls off his bedroom wall in the middle of the night.

And when they pull the bulletin board off him, he's as thin as a piece of paper.

I thought it was pretty cool that Flat Stanley could fold himself up and get mailed to his grandma's, or have his brother fly him like a kite.

But I'll tell you this: If Flat Stanley had a brother like RODRICK, I guarantee he wouldn't survive a whole day.

I really liked the book, but it kind of freaked me out, too. One thing it did was give me a deathly fear of bulletin boards.

In second grade, everyone in my class had to color in a cutout of Flat Stanley and mail him to a friend or relative who lived far away.

Then that person was supposed to take a picture of Flat Stanley in front of something interesting and mail him back with the photo.

My friend Rowley sent Flat Stanley to a bunch of his relatives and got lots of cool pictures back. Rowley even sent him to his uncle who lives in Asia, and he took a picture of Flat Stanley in front of the Great Wall of China.

Well, the first person Mom sent MY Flat Stanley to was her cousin Stacey, who lives out in Seattle. But she probably wasn't the best choice.

Stacey is one of those people who hoard all sorts of stuff, like newspapers and magazines, so Mom should've known that once her cousin got her hands on Flat Stanley he wasn't coming back.

Today, Mom said she was gonna take photos of our new Flat Stanley in front of all the cool places we visit and then make a scrapbook of our trip. And as soon as we got on the highway, she started snapping pictures. But she was probably a little too eager, because her first few pictures weren't exactly keepers.

When Mom wasn't taking pictures, Flat Stanley was taped to the front air-conditioning vent. All I can say is, he was having a lot better ride than I was. The windows in the back of the van don't open, and the vents were blocked by all our luggage, so I wasn't getting ANY cold air.

What made me even MORE uncomfortable was the fact that Mom was in control of the trip. Mom always tries to make things about education, and I knew she was gonna turn this experience into one long lesson.

She's been doing that ever since I was little. I remember when I got scratched by Gramma's cat and Mom tried to turn it into a "teaching moment."

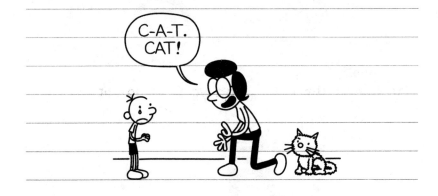

C-A-T. CAT!

Sure enough, a half hour into the trip today, Mom started in with the educational stuff.

She had borrowed a bunch of CDs from the library that teach Spanish, and said we'd use the long stretches on the road to learn a new language as a family.

Mom's always saying that learning a foreign language is the best thing you can do for your brain. That might be true, but I think she should leave the actual TEACHING to the schools.

Mom decided it would be a good idea to expose me to a foreign language early on, so when I was in first grade, she would put the Spanish-speaking channels on TV while we ate breakfast.

Mom would repeat whatever they said on the television, but when SHE said the words they came out a little bit different.

I ended up learning all sorts of phrases that weren't right. For example, the way you're SUPPOSED to say "What's your name" in Spanish is "Cómo te llamas." Well, I know that NOW because I learned it in my middle school Spanish class.

But when I was little, Mom taught me that "What's your name" in Spanish is "Te amo," which ACTUALLY means "I love you." I just wish I had known that before I said it to a million different people.

Today, Mom played the first two Spanish CDs, but she got frustrated that no one seemed to be paying attention. So she switched gears and said we were gonna play a car game she read about in her magazine.

The game was called Alphabet Groceries, and you play it like this: The first player has to name an item you can get at the grocery store that starts with the letter "A." The next person has to come up with an item that starts with "B," and so on.

If a player CAN'T come up with an item that starts with their letter, they're out of the game.

Mom said I should go first, so I said "apple," which I guess was kind of an obvious choice. Rodrick was up next, but he said he couldn't come up with any food that started with "B."

I'm pretty sure he was lying to get out of having to play the game, but with Rodrick, you never know.

When Rodrick got knocked out, the turn went to Manny, who came up with his word right away.

Mom started clapping, but I pointed out that "bapple" isn't a real word. She said Manny is just learning the alphabet and that we all need to "encourage" him.

I quit in protest, and from then on it was only Manny, Mom, and Dad playing. I really wished my earplugs weren't buried in my duffel bag under a pile of suitcases, because the next hour and a half was pretty painful.

All that talk of food was actually getting me kind of hungry, and when I saw a sign for a drive-through place at the next exit, I asked Mom if we could pull over. But Mom said we wouldn't be stopping at any of THOSE kinds of restaurants, because they don't serve "real food."

She said fast-food places lure kids in with cheap plastic toys to trick them into eating sugar and fat, and we weren't gonna fall into that trap. Mom said she had a MUCH better alternative and handed me a lunch bag with my name on it.

Mom said she got the Mommy Meal idea from "Family Frolic," which I guess should not have come as a surprise.

Inside the bag was a tuna fish sandwich, an orange, and a little carton of milk, plus something wrapped in tinfoil.

Mom said I had to eat my fruit before I unwrapped the tinfoil, because that was my "prize."

But I wish I had just opened it right away, because I wouldn't have eaten the whole orange if I'd known the prize was a pack of math flash cards.

Rodrick got flash cards in HIS lunch, too, and we could both see where this was headed. So before Mom could turn the next hour of the trip into a tutoring session, I pulled out one of the games Mom had packed in a big tote bag.

The game I grabbed was called "I Must Confess," and when Mom saw it she got so excited she forgot all about the flash cards.

I read the rules, which were pretty simple: One person takes a card from the deck and reads it out loud to everyone else.

I Must Confess...

... I'VE MET A FAMOUS PERSON.

If one of the players has done the thing that's written on the card, they earn a point. And the first player to get ten points wins.

I was a little skeptical at first, but I have to admit, the game was actually kind of FUN. I learned a lot of things about Mom and Dad I never knew before.

I found out that Dad had a pet chameleon when
he was a kid and that Mom dyed her hair blond
once, which really surprised me.

Believe it or not, even RODRICK was getting
into the game. He got a point for being the only
person who'd ever slept out overnight for tickets
to a concert, and ANOTHER point for getting
a bug stuck in his ear, which I remember like it
was yesterday.

Dad and Rodrick were neck and neck with nine points, and whoever scored next would win the game. Mom seemed really happy everyone was getting along and having fun.

Then she pulled a new card out of the deck and read it.

I MUST CONFESS I'VE TOILET-PAPERED A NEIGHBOR'S HOUSE!

I'm pretty sure Mom thought no one was gonna get a point on that card, because she was already reaching for the next one. But Rodrick started acting like he had just won the lottery.

I WIN!
I WIN!

Mom thought Rodrick was lying to get a point, but he told her it was TRUE. He said that a few months ago, he and his bandmates toilet-papered Mrs. Tuttle's house next door after she called the police to complain they were making too much noise rehearsing.

Rodrick thought the whole thing was pretty funny, but Mom didn't seem amused.

LET ME GET THIS STRAIGHT: YOU AND TWO OF YOUR BANDMATES TOILET-PAPERED AN ELDERLY WOMAN'S HOUSE?

If I was Rodrick, I would've changed my story real quick and said I was just joking around to win the game. But Rodrick didn't seize his chance to bail out.

Mom had Dad pull over to the side of the road, then handed Rodrick her phone and made him call Mrs. Tuttle to apologize, which was awkward for everyone in the car.

After that, it was quiet in the van for a long time. Mom was about to pop the next Spanish CD in the stereo, but luckily Manny had fallen asleep by then, so she couldn't.

If you wake Manny up in the middle of one of his naps, he'll go completely ballistic, and there's NO calming him down. So whenever Manny falls asleep, Mom and Dad do everything they can to KEEP him that way.

I was big on naps when I was Manny's age, too. I used to take an hour-long nap after lunch every day, and when I started preschool, we had an official nap time where everyone pulled out a mat and slept on the floor.

If you ask me, I think they should give kids nap time all the way through college. But they stop doing it after preschool, which I found out the HARD way.

On the first day of kindergarten, after we had our snacks, I asked the teacher where the mats were, so we could lie down and recharge our batteries.

But she said kindergartners don't HAVE nap time, and I thought she was just making a funny joke.

A few minutes later the whole class was making
paper bag puppets. Apparently, I was the only
one who didn't get the heads-up about the no-nap
thing, because for the rest of the day everyone
else seemed fine, while I could barely function.

TRUDGE
TRUDGE

I'm glad Mom remembered to bring a pacifier on
the trip, because as long as Manny's got one stuck
in his mouth, he can sleep through just about
anything. Manny lost his favorite pacifier last
night, but Dad ran out to get a new one at a
store near our house that sells gag gifts.

I guess it looks a little strange, but it works just as well as a regular one.

Manny had been sleeping peacefully for about an hour today when we stopped at a tollbooth. Dad rolled down his window to get a ticket, and the guy in the booth had such a loud voice he sounded like he was speaking through a MEGAPHONE.

Manny started to fuss, and his pacifier came halfway out of his mouth. But luckily Rodrick reacted quickly, and Manny fell back asleep.

I think Mom was a little frustrated that Manny was napping in the first place. She had marked a bunch of places on her map where she wanted us to stop and get out for some sightseeing, but now we had to keep driving.

The problem I had with Manny's nap was that I really needed to get out of the car and stretch, but I COULDN'T.

I tried to make myself comfortable, but with all the stuff piled around me, it was impossible.

Luckily, my backpack was in arm's reach behind my seat, because it had some books and other things I'd brought to entertain myself.

Mom's always trying to get me to read stuff that's "enriching," but when it comes to books, I know what I like. And ever since elementary school, my favorite books have been the ones in the Underpants Bandits series.

The Underpants Bandits books are about these two kids named Bryce and Brody who go back in time and steal underwear from famous people so they can put the underpants in a museum.

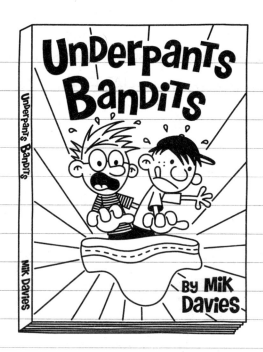

I know that sounds kind of ridiculous, but the books are actually pretty funny.

And just as Van Gogh returned to his masterpiece, Bryce snatched the painter's favorite pair of boxers, which, thank goodness, were clean.

The books are super popular with boys at my school, but the teachers HATE them because of all the "rude humor."

Whenever a book report was due in fifth grade, all the boys in my class did theirs on one of the Underpants Bandits books. And that made my teacher, Mrs. Terry, hate them even MORE.

Our class had a project where we had to write a letter to our favorite author, and of course all the boys chose Mik Davies.

But Mrs. Terry said we had to pick someone ELSE, so I grabbed a random book from the library and wrote my letter to an author I'd never even heard of before.

March 30th

Dear Nathaniel,

My teacher made us write to an author, so I picked you. I have not read any of your books (no offense).

Here are my questions for you:

1. What's your favorite color?

2. What's your favorite animal?

3. What's your favorite flavor of ice cream?

4. What's your favorite super-hero movie?

I would appreciate it if you could answer me soon, because I am getting graded on this.

Sincerely,

Greg Heffley

But I probably should've checked the year the book was written before I wrote my letter.

May 20th

Dear Mr. Heffley,

We regret to inform you that the author to whom you have written, Mr. Hawthorne, passed away more than a century ago.

As such, he will not be able to respond to your questions.

With regrets,

Katrina Welker
Publisher

Most PARENTS don't like the Underpants Bandits books, either.

In fact, the PTA had a meeting that year where they decided parents' tax dollars shouldn't be used to purchase any of the Underpants Bandits books for the library.

When we came back to school from spring break, all of the Underpants Bandits books in the library were GONE.

I hope these adults are happy when a whole generation of boys grow up not knowing how to read.

When the school banned the Underpants Bandits books, it just made them more popular than EVER. Some boys snuck in copies from home and passed them on to OTHER kids.

One kid even brought in a bootleg copy of an Underpants Bandits book from Japan. I couldn't understand a word of it, but it was pretty easy to figure out from the pictures what was going on.

I actually wrote to the author on my OWN just
to tell him how much I liked his series.

August 18th

Dear Mr. Davies,

I'm just writing to tell you, don't listen to
these people who say your books are
garbage, because they don't know what
they're talking about. I know a bunch
of kids (including me) who think your
books are great.

As far as the "rude humor" goes, I find
that stuff hilarious, so please don't
change a thing. In fact, I would
encourage you to put MORE bodily
functions and things of that nature in
your books.

Sincerely,

Greg Heffley

I'd never written a fan letter like that, and every
day when I got home from school, I ran to the
mailbox to see if Mik Davies had written me back.

I finally got a response almost a year later, and
I was really excited.

But when I read the letter, it was a HUGE
disappointment.

From The DesK OF
MiK Davies

Dear friend,

Unfortunately, I get so much fan mail
that I'm not able to answer your letter
personally.

But I did want to tell you to be on the
lookout for "Underpants Bandits 24:
Lincoln's Longjohns," coming soon to
stores near you!

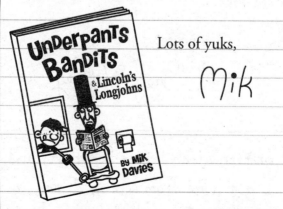

UnDerPanTs
BanDiTs
& Lincoln's
Longjohns

BY MiK
Davies

Lots of yuks,

Mik

I couldn't believe I poured my heart out to this guy and all I got back was an AD.

Even though that whole experience left a bad taste in my mouth, I still like his books.

At least I get to read whatever I WANT this summer. Rodrick's school gave him a whole list for required reading, and some of the books look like a lot of work.

But Rodrick's not much of a reader, so he rented all the MOVIE versions of the books on his list.

Mom said it's not smart to watch the movie without reading the book, because they usually change a lot of stuff. But Rodrick said as long as he got the basic idea, he'd be fine.

I think his approach is gonna cause problems, though. "The Lord of the Rings" is on his summer reading list, but when he rented the movie, he wasn't careful about checking the title.

Rodrick watched the movie TWICE, and after the second time he told Mom that whoever wrote the book must be a genius. But I'm guessing Rodrick's teacher is gonna be pretty confused when she reads his book report in September.

By the time I was done reading today, I really needed to get out of the car to prevent my legs from permanently cramping.

Manny was still asleep, but he had somehow turned himself all the way upside down in his seat.

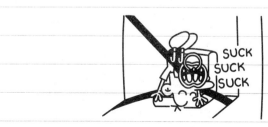

When Mom noticed, she told Dad maybe we should stop driving for the day, so he pulled off at the next exit.

I was really looking forward to eating a meal at a decent restaurant, but Mom said we're on a budget and tonight we were gonna pick up our dinner at a grocery store.

Dad found a supermarket a few miles from the exit. But Mom was afraid that if the van stopped moving, Manny would wake up and have a fit. So Mom wrote out a shopping list for Rodrick and gave him some money, then Dad drove real slow in front of the entrance so Rodrick could hop out.

Dad had to circle the parking lot about ten times, which wasn't easy since we were towing a boat. Eventually, Rodrick came out with a couple bags of groceries. And from the looks of it, he picked up some extra items for himself.

When Dad pulled the van around, Rodrick hopped in. Then we started looking for a place to stay for the night, but the selection in the area wasn't that great.

A few of the motels had big signs that said
they had "Color TV," which if you ask me is not
anything to brag about in this day and age.

Dad finally pulled over at a place with air-
conditioning and a pool, which sounded pretty
good to me, especially considering that I'd lost
about five pounds in sweat sitting in the backseat.

I haven't stayed in a whole lot of motels, but if
I had to guess, I'd say we picked one on the
lower end of the spectrum.

The lobby smelled like mildew, and the carpet was
covered in weird stains.

But everyone was too tired to get back in the car and look for another place to stay.

We got the key to our room, and when we walked in it reeked of smoke. There were little holes in the comforter and pillows that I'm pretty sure were cigarette burns.

Dad picked a towel off the floor, then dropped it because it was WET.

Mom went back to the front desk and asked for a different room, but the clerk said the motel was full and that we'd gotten the last one.

Mom told her in that case we were gonna leave and take our business to another motel. But the clerk told her there was a twenty-four-hour cancellation policy, so we couldn't get our money back.

When Mom returned to the room, she said we were gonna have to try and make the best of a bad situation. Then she and Dad stripped the bed down to the bare mattress.

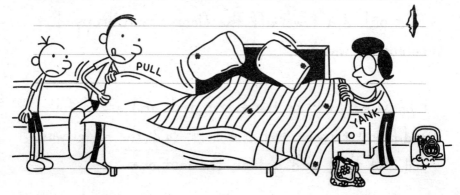

Believe it or not, Manny slept through ALL of this. Mom said that if he woke up now, he'd be awake all night, so she was just gonna let him sleep through till morning.

Mom put Manny down in the middle of the sofa bed and pulled a blanket over him.

The rest of us were really hungry, so we emptied out the groceries Rodrick bought. But it turned out he didn't buy ANYTHING on Mom's list.

Rodrick was supposed to get sandwich supplies, orange juice, and stuff like that, but he just got a bunch of things HE likes.

Mom was pretty upset that Rodrick didn't get a single thing on the list she gave him, but his excuse was that he couldn't read her handwriting. Mom told him it wasn't very smart to get cinnamon rolls and a frozen pizza, since those things needed an oven and we didn't HAVE one.

But Rodrick said we could MICROWAVE the pizza. Then he put it inside the microwave oven to prove it.

At least, Rodrick THOUGHT it was a microwave. It was actually a SAFE. By the time he figured that out, the pizza was locked inside.

Mom gave me what was left of her cash and said to go down to the vending machine to get the most nutritious stuff I could find.

And that's how we ended up eating sugar wafers and breath mints for dinner on the first night of our road trip.

Sunday

Last night we couldn't watch TV or do anything in the room because Manny was asleep on the pullout sofa.

Mom wouldn't even let us keep the light on, so we all sat in the dark for a while until me and Rodrick decided to go down to the pool to kill some time.

Well, the sign outside the motel said there was a pool, but there was no actual WATER in it.

And it didn't look like there HAD been for at least five years.

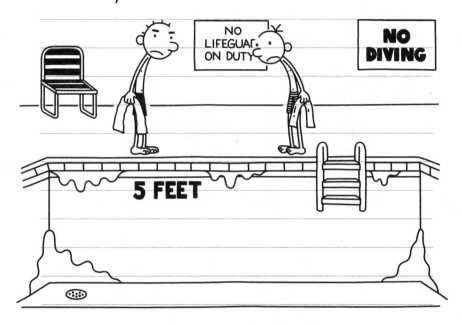

There was a hot tub near the pool that DID have water in it, but some family was already using it. So me and Rodrick waited our turn.

Unfortunately, the family couldn't take a hint that we wanted to use the hot tub, so eventually me and Rodrick just went back to the room.

The lights were still out, and Mom and Dad were asleep on the mattress. I guess they must've been pretty exhausted, because they were still wearing all their clothes.

With Mom and Dad on the bed and Manny on the sofa, it didn't leave a lot of good sleep options for me and Rodrick.

We checked the closet for a cot or an air mattress, but there was nothing.

Rodrick was one step ahead of me, though. He gathered up the sofa cushions and made a bed for himself on the floor. Five seconds later, he was out cold.

I figured the closet was as good a place as any for me to sleep, so I got some towels out of the bathroom and laid them on the floor.

After lying there for a minute, I noticed a TERRIBLE smell and thought a mouse must've died in the vent or something.

I tried covering my nose with a washcloth, but that seemed to make the smell even WORSE.

It was hard enough trying to fall asleep under those conditions, but then someone in the room started SNORING. Luckily, I was prepared for that. Mom and Dad BOTH snore, which is the reason I thought ahead and brought earplugs on the trip.

But it was so dark in the room I could only find ONE in my duffel bag, so I had to try sleeping with the earplug in my left ear and my other ear pressed to the floor.

I did actually fall asleep for a few minutes, but woke up to some kind of ruckus going on outside.

When I looked out the peephole, I saw something flash by, but I couldn't tell what it was. So I cracked open the door to see what was going on.

It turns out those kids from the hot tub had gotten their hands on a cleaning cart and were ramming it into a wall.

I couldn't BELIEVE these kids' parents were letting them run wild in the middle of the night, so I stepped out of the room and went over to give them a piece of my mind.

The littlest kid burst into tears and ran into his room, and I didn't feel bad for even one second. But a minute later his door opened again, and his FATHER came out.

I wasn't about to get yelled at by a grown man in his underwear, so I ran back to our room and locked the door. Then I prayed with all my might that the chain lock was strong enough to keep him out.

I guess the kids' dad didn't see which door I went into, because he knocked on the wrong one. Then he pounded on the door right next to ours before giving up and going back to his room.

Once the coast was clear, I hung a little sign on our doorknob in case the guy decided to come BACK.

It was REALLY hard falling asleep after that, because every time I heard someone outside the door, I held my breath until they passed by.

Before I knew it, the sun was up and so was Manny. Mom turned on the television, and whenever Manny watches TV, he TALKS to it.

I was a little annoyed with Manny blabbering away, but I guess I can't complain. I used to do the same exact thing when I was younger.

One time when I was watching my favorite show, the host asked a question.

I was just goofing around when I answered, but the guy on TV actually RESPONDED.

I wish it never happened, though. Because for a long time after that, I thought the people inside the TV could hear everything I said.

In fact, on my sixth birthday, Mom had to sit me down and have a talk about the difference between "imaginary" friends and "real" friends.

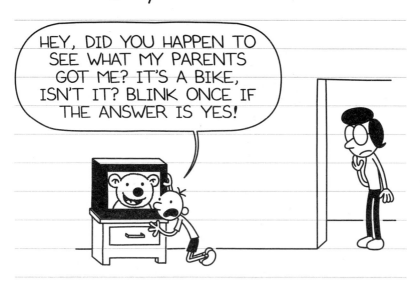

HEY, DID YOU HAPPEN TO SEE WHAT MY PARENTS GOT ME? IT'S A BIKE, ISN'T IT? BLINK ONCE IF THE ANSWER IS YES!

Once Manny got going in a conversation with his favorite TV characters this morning, I knew there was no point in trying to fall back asleep. So I just got up for the day.

And when I did, I found out the source of that awful smell. Rodrick had put his shoes in the closet, and I had spent the whole night breathing in his fumes.

But even WORSE was that the "washcloth" I had used to block the smell was actually one of Rodrick's SOCKS.

Speaking of Rodrick, Manny's conversation with the TV didn't bother him one little bit, because he just slept right through all the noise.

CAN YOU HOP LIKE A FROG?

HOP! HOP!

Dad was getting a little restless waiting for everyone to get going this morning. He's one of those guys who gets up every day at the crack of dawn so he can arrive at his office early, and this whole late-start thing wasn't working for him.

Eventually, Mom made Rodrick get up and take a shower. We went to a diner right next to the motel for breakfast, then got back in the van.

Mom said that from now on we were all gonna be on the same sleep schedule so we wouldn't waste any more time on our trip. But before she was even done talking, Manny passed out in his car seat.

Mom's big plan for the day was for us to go to a country fair she read about in "Family Frolic."

I'd never been to anything like that before, but it looked like it was worth checking out.

The fair was a few hours away, so that meant me being cramped in the backseat again, which was starting to get old. Thankfully, after an hour, Mom offered to switch places with me.

When I got up to the front seat, I couldn't believe how much ROOM there was.

And it wasn't just all the space that was awesome. I even had individual temperature settings and my own cup holder.

I went to change the radio station, but Dad stopped me. He said only the DRIVER gets to pick the music. I didn't think that was fair, but I wasn't gonna complain and risk getting sent to the backseat.

♪ MY TRUCK IS BUSTED BUT ♪ ♫ MY DOG HE LOVES ME ♫

Dad's music was pretty awful, but the view totally made up for it.

When you're in the back, you don't have any sense of what's ahead. Sitting up front, I had a whole new perspective and could almost see why Mom was so gung ho about taking this road trip.

When we took the exit for the country fair, we came to a stoplight. We were behind a minivan that was the same exact model as ours, only purple.

The kids in the van looked kind of familiar. It took me a second to realize they were the same ones from last night.

I hadn't told Mom and Dad about the incident with the kids and the cleaning cart, because I was worried I wouldn't come out looking too great. And they definitely didn't need to know about my run-in with Mr. Beardo.

The kids in the purple van recognized me right away, and started making obnoxious faces.

I wasn't gonna just sit there and take it from those little punks, so I made a face at THEM.

The skinny one made the same face back at ME, and the second he did, the light turned green and they accelerated. When their van lurched forward, the little kid face-planted into the back window.

Dad passed them on the left, and Mr. Beardo got a real good look at me.

Luckily, the parking lot for the fair was only a few hundred feet up the road. Once we stopped, I wanted to stay inside until I was sure we weren't being tailed by the purple van.

But it looked like we were in the clear. Manny was still asleep in his car seat, so Mom said she'd stay back with him and the rest of us could go on ahead.

The fair was a LOT different than I thought it was gonna be. I expected it to have a Ferris wheel and a merry-go-round and stuff like that, but instead there were a bunch of tents with farm animals and booths with homemade food.

We were getting kind of hungry anyway, so we went looking for something to eat.

They had corn dogs and fried dough and all the stuff you'd expect at a big fair. But then they had crazy things like deep-fried butter on a stick.

I was actually glad Mom was still in the van, because I was pretty sure that kind of thing didn't qualify as "real food" in her book.

After about an hour of walking the fairgrounds, Dad went back to the car to see if Manny was awake yet, and he told me and Rodrick to go explore on our own.

The two of us wandered around for a while until we came across a tent where there was something big going on.

It was a Foulest Footwear contest, and they were offering a prize for whoever had the nastiest shoe.

There was a big line of people ready to submit their entries.

FOULEST FOOTWEAR
CONTEST

I told Rodrick HE should enter, because if ANYONE deserved to win this thing, it was him.

While we were waiting in line, me and Rodrick got in an argument over who would get to keep the prize. I said we should split it 50-50 because it was my idea, but he said he should get the whole thing because it was HIS shoe and he was the one who made it stink.

Right before we got to the judging table, we reached a compromise where I'd get 10% of the prize as Rodrick's agent.

Some of the other shoes looked a lot worse than Rodrick's, and I was losing confidence that he'd win. But when the judges got to the smell test, it was all over.

Rodrick won first prize, which turned out to be a coupon for one deep-fried butter on a stick. I told Rodrick he could have it all to himself, because the thought of eating any more butter made me feel a little nauseous.

Rodrick asked the judges for his shoe back, but they said they were gonna send it on to the national competition. So that left Rodrick walking around with only one shoe. I decided to explore the nearby stalls while Rodrick was polishing off his stick of fried butter.

But I had a SERIOUSLY close call when I turned a corner and almost ran smack into the entire Beardo family. Luckily, I was able to duck for cover just in time.

Now that I knew the Beardos were on the fairgrounds, I was eager to get out of there.

I went to look for Rodrick, but he must've gone back to the van. I decided to head there myself, but on my way out I spotted the top of Mom's head in a crowd under one of the livestock tents.

People were packed shoulder to shoulder, and I tried pushing my way through to get to where Mom was.

But when I got halfway in, a big cheer went up.

When I finally made it up to the front, I was surprised to see Manny standing in the middle of the crowd, holding a piece of paper.

Apparently, there was a contest to see who could come the closest to guessing the weight of a hog, and Manny got it exactly right.

The prize for guessing the hog's weight was a real live baby pig.

Mom explained to the judge that they'd just entered the contest for fun and didn't actually WANT the pig.

But the people in the crowd seemed kind of insulted and wouldn't take no for an answer.

With all the commotion this was causing, I was nervous the Beardo family was gonna come over to the livestock tent to see what was going on. Luckily, by then Mom seemed ready to get out of there herself, and we made our way to the exit.

Dad was sitting in the van with the air-conditioning cranked up, and when he saw Mom carrying a pig, he was a little taken by surprise.

Mom filled Dad in on how Manny won the pig in the contest, but he didn't seem too thrilled with the news.

Dad said we had no business owning a pig and that we needed to take it back to the fair immediately.

But Mom said it was too late, because the pig had already "imprinted" on Manny.

Dad still wasn't on board, though. He said a pig is a "barn animal" and could be carrying all sorts of parasites and whatnot. But Mom said a LOT of people keep pigs as pets, and she'd heard they're just as smart as dogs.

Then Rodrick got in on the conversation. He voted for KEEPING the pig because he said we could get free bacon from it every morning, the way you get eggs from a chicken.

So either he doesn't understand how pigs work, or he just wasn't thinking it all the way through.

I was all in favor of keeping the pig if it meant we could hurry up and get going.

I noticed a purple van parked a few spaces away from ours, and I was nervous the Beardos would show up any second.

Dad finally caved in. He said if we were gonna keep the pig, it would have to ride in the boat. But Mom said putting the pig in the boat was "inhumane" and that we needed to find a place for it in the van.

The thing is, there wasn't anywhere to PUT the pig in the van. We couldn't just let it roam free, and we couldn't exactly strap it in with a seat belt, either. So Mom emptied out the cooler and put the pig in THERE.

Once that was settled, we finally pulled out of the parking lot.

After we put a few miles between us and the fair,
I could finally breathe again.

But the pig started causing trouble right away.
By the time we got back on the highway, it had
tipped over the cooler and was rooting around in
one of the Mommy Meal bags.

SNUFFLE
GRUNT
SLORK

I had to wrangle the pig back into the cooler,
and THIS time I strapped the seat belt across
it so it wouldn't tip over.

Mom figured the pig was hungry, so she said we
needed to stop and get it some food. Her idea
was for us to go to a restaurant and then give
the pig our leftovers. That sounded like a good
deal to me, since it meant we'd actually get to
have a sit-down dinner.

We found a place to eat a few miles away, and Mom stayed back in the van with the pig while the rest of us went inside. But when the waitress saw that Rodrick was only wearing one shoe, she said she couldn't serve him.

Dad said me and Rodrick could take turns using MY shoe. But I wish I hadn't let Rodrick go first, because he's the world's slowest eater.

When we got back in the van, we gave the pig our leftover corn and vegetables, which it ate straight out of the styrofoam container.

Mom started looking up places to stay for the night on the GPS. She asked Rodrick to call a hotel to see if they had any rooms available. They did, but Rodrick blew it by getting too specific.

Mom found another place a few miles away, and this time she did the talking.

The hotel was just after the tolls. A few hundred feet from the exit, traffic came to a crawl.

That was a problem for me because I had two big glasses of lemonade at the restaurant and REALLY needed to use the bathroom.

I spotted a gas station up ahead and asked Mom and Dad if I could hop out and use the bathroom, then catch up with the car after I was done.

Dad didn't like the idea because he was worried that by the time I got back, they might already be through the tollbooth. By now it was pretty obvious the pig needed to go, too, because it was running in little circles inside the cooler.

Mom said I could use the bathroom at the gas station as long as I brought the pig WITH me.

So I tucked it under my arm and ran across three lanes of traffic to the gas station.

I tried the handle to the men's room, but it was locked. I waited for the person using it to come OUT, but whoever was in there wasn't in any rush to wrap things up.

I was getting kind of desperate, so I tried the handle to the women's room, but THAT was locked, too.

I ran back to the car, which had only moved forward about five feet in the time I was gone.

When I told Mom that both bathrooms were occupied, she said gas station bathrooms are ALWAYS locked and that I had to ask the ATTENDANT for the key.

So I ran BACK to the gas station and told the guy at the desk I needed to use the restroom in a hurry.

I'm not sure what I was expecting from a gas station bathroom, but it was actually a lot WORSE than I could've even imagined.

Let me just say it was pretty awkward using the toilet with a farm animal staring right at me. But the pig was even MORE embarrassed than I was, because when it was the pig's turn to go, nothing happened.

After I gave the key back to the attendant,
I spotted our van just as it was about to go
through the tollbooth. So I sprinted all the way
across traffic to get to it in time.

But before I opened the door, I wish I had
noticed that the van didn't have a BOAT
attached to it.

OUR van was actually still a few cars back, and
by the time I got inside, the pig looked like he
was about to burst.

I guess Mom was right about pigs being smart,
because when I put him on Manny's potty seat,
he knew EXACTLY what to do.

ACKNOWLEDGMENTS

Thanks to my wonderful family for your continued love, support, and encouragement.

Thanks to everyone at Abrams for treating every Wimpy Kid book like it's the first. Thanks especially to Charlie Kochman, Michael Jacobs, Jason Wells, Veronica Wasserman, Steve Tager, Susan Van Metre, Jen Graham, Chad W. Beckerman, Alison Gervais, Elisa Garcia, Erica La Sala, and Scott Auerbach.

Thanks to all my international publishers for bringing Greg's stories to kids all over the world. I feel very grateful for the friendships I've made over the past few years.

Thanks to Shaelyn Germain and Anna Cesary for everything you do to keep all the balls in the air at the same time.

Thanks to Paul Sennott and Ike Williams for all the great advice.

Thanks to everyone in Hollywood who has worked to bring Greg Heffley to life on the big and small screens. Thanks especially to Sylvie Rabineau, Keith Fleer, Nina Jacobson, Brad Simpson, Ralph Milero, Roland Poindexter, Elizabeth Gabler, and Vanessa Morrison.

Thanks to everyone at Poptropica, especially Jess Brallier.

ABOUT THE AUTHOR

Jeff Kinney is a #1 *New York Times* bestselling author and four-time Nickelodeon Kids' Choice Award winner for Favorite Book. Jeff has been named one of *Time* magazine's 100 Most Influential People in the World. He is also the creator of Poptropica, which was named one of *Time* magazine's 50 Best Websites. He spent his childhood in the Washington, D.C., area and moved to New England in 1995. Jeff lives with his wife and two sons in southern Massachusetts, where he is opening a bookstore.

杰夫·金尼 中国行

Jeff Kinney's Visit to China

2015年对中国的"哈屁族"来说，是具有划时代意义的一年！因为《小屁孩日记》的作者杰夫·金尼终于掘出了他童年梦想中的那条地道，从美国到地球另一边的中国来啦！

北京是"杰夫·金尼2015全球巡回活动"的第4站。2015年11月4日，以扁平娃斯坦利为首的一众小编终于在北京首都国际机场迎来了"小屁孩之父"杰夫·金尼！

主角登场！

接下来的11月5日，重头戏轮番上演啦！

★ 杰夫叔叔先是参加了《小屁孩日记》中文版发行600万册的庆祝会，并在会上宣布了他的新书出版计划。

大家要关注《小屁孩日记》的新书哟！

中国儿童文学作家颜值都那么高吗？（设计对白）

★ 然后，他跟中国著名儿童文学作家"阳光姐姐"伍美珍就中美少儿课外阅读情况展开了对谈。

杰夫叔叔原来也好亲切呀！（设计对白）

★ 活动现场也来了很多"哈屁族"，自然少不了签书环节，《小屁孩日记》真是大小通吃呢！

★ 不少书迷一拿到书就迫不及待地看了起来，你看，头都要扎到书里去啦！

★ 杰夫叔叔还收获了"哈屁族"送的一大堆礼物。这位小读者好有心思呀，让杰夫叔叔认识了自己的中文名。

★ 11月5日下午，杰夫叔叔还到当当网的总部接受了访谈，回答了很多有趣的问题，例如：

主持人：通过今天上午的接触，您觉得中国的小读者跟您想象的小读者是一样的吗？

我觉得全球的孩子都是一样的，他们都有父母、兄弟姐妹、有宠物和老师，所以这就是我的书为什么能受到这些孩子欢迎的原因，因为世界各地的孩子们的童年是有很多共通之处的。

主持人：因为这本书里面的事情太逼真了，会让人觉得很多事情是不是发生在您自己小时候，或者发生在您孩子的身上？

这些故事大部分其实都是有一些真人真事的依据的，然后根据这些事进行的改编。比如说我刚才随手翻开一页，这一页描述的是，格雷在院子里面找他祖母的戒指。这个故事确有其事⋯⋯

篇幅有限，未能尽录。

好玩的问题还有很多呢，大家一定还想看看杰夫叔叔的回答吧？不要着急，只要关注"新世纪童书绘"的微信公众号（搜索"xsjpublish"，或扫描右手边的二维码），在对话框输入"小屁孩"并发送，就可以看到这次访谈的全部内容啦！

★ 11月5日晚上，杰夫叔叔来到北京西单图书大厦，跟广大读者见面，还给大家示范了"小屁孩"格雷的画法。

★ 活动结束后，杰夫叔叔还没能休息哦！他被带到一堆"书山"前面，这是要干什么呢？

当然是为广大读者谋福利啦！你们想要的亲笔签名本，就是从这个"深夜流水线"上扒下来的。

立刻关注全国各大书店及各大网络书店的动态，即有机会获得杰夫·金尼亲笔签名的《小屁孩日记》。

★ 11月6日，杰夫叔叔终于如愿来到了神秘又古老的故宫。

好兴奋！可以跟杰夫叔叔同游故宫耶！（设计对白）

好兴奋！终于到故宫啦！（设计对白）

又被读者逮住索要签名了。

跟扁平娃斯坦利来张合照吧！茄子！

杰夫叔叔短短两天的中国之旅就这样愉快地结束啦！你们想再见到他吗？想他到你的城市去吗？赶快关注"新世纪童书绘"的微信公众号（搜索"xsjpublish"，或扫描前页的二维码）和"小屁孩日记官方微博"（http://weibo.com/wimpywimpy），或者打电话到020-83795744，把你们的愿望告诉小编吧！

望子快乐

朱子庆

在一个人的一生中，"与有荣焉"的机会或有，但肯定不多。因为儿子译了一部畅销书，而老爸被邀涂鸦几句，像这样的与荣，我想，即使放眼天下，也没有几人领得吧。

儿子接活儿翻译《小屁孩日记》时，还在读着大三。这是安安他第一次领译书稿，多少有点紧张和兴奋吧，起初他每译几段，便"飞鸽传书"，不一会儿人也跟过来，在我面前"项庄舞剑"地问："有意思么？有意思么？"怎么当时我就没有作乐不可支状呢？于今想来，我竟很有些后悔。对于一个喂饱段子与小品的中国人，若说还有什么洋幽默能令我们"绝倒"，难！不过，安安译成杀青之时，图文并茂，我得以从头到尾再读一遍，我得当说，这部书岂止有意思呢，读了它使我有一种冲动，假如时间可以倒流，我很想尝试重新做一回父亲！我不免窃想，安安在译它的时候，不知会怎样腹诽我这个老爸呢！

我宁愿儿子是书里那个小屁孩！

你可能会说，你别是在做秀吧，小屁孩格雷将来能出息成个什么样子，实在还很难说……这个质疑，典型地出诸一个中国人之口，出之于为父母的中国人之口。望子成龙，一定要孩子出息成个什么样子，虽说初衷也是为了孩子，但最终却是苦了孩子。"生年不满百，常怀千岁忧。"现在，由于这深重的忧患，我们已经把成功学启示的模式都做到胎教了！而望子快乐，有谁想过？从小就快乐，快乐一生？惭愧，我也是看了《小屁孩日记》才想到这点，然而儿子已不再年少！我觉得很有些对不住儿子！

我从来没有对安安的"少年老成"感到过有什么不妥，毕竟少年老成使人放心。而今读其译作而被触动，此心才为之不安起来。我在想，比起美国的小屁孩格雷和他的同学们，我们中国的小屁孩们是不是活得不很小屁孩？是不是普遍地过于负重、乏乐和少年老成？而当他们将来长大，娶妻（嫁夫）生子（女），为人父母，会不会还要循此逻辑再造下一代？想想安安少年时，起早贪黑地读书、写作业，小四眼，十足一个书呆子，类似格雷那样的调皮、贪玩、小有恶搞、缰绳牢笼不住地敢于尝试和行动主义……太缺少了。印象中，安安最突出的一次，也就是读小学三年级时，做了一回带头大哥，拔了校园里所有自行车的气门芯并四处派发，仅此而已吧（此处请在家长指导下阅读）。

说点别的吧。中国作家写的儿童文学作品，很少能引发成年读者的阅读兴趣。安徒生童话之所以风靡天下，在于它征服了成年读者。在我看来，《小屁孩日记》也属于成人少年兼宜的读物，可以父子同修！谁没有年少轻狂？谁没有豆蔻年华？只不过呢，对于为父母者，阅读它，会使你由会心一笑而再笑，继以感慨系之，进而不免有所自省，对照和检讨一下自己和孩子的关系，以及在某些类似事情的处理上，自己是否欠妥？等等。它虽系成人所作，书中对孩子心性的把握，却准确传神；虽非心理学著作，对了解孩子的心理和行为，也不无参悟和启示。品学兼优和顽劣不学的孩子毕竟是少数，小屁孩格雷是"中间人物"的一个玲珑典型，着实招人怜爱——在格雷身上，有着我们彼此都难免有的各样小心思、小算计、小毛病，就好像阿Q，读来透着与我们有那么一种割不断的血缘关系，这，也许就是此书在美国乃至全球都特别畅销的原因吧！

最后我想申明的是，第一读者身份在我是弥足珍惜的，因为，宝贝儿子出生时，第一眼看见他的是医生，老爸都摊不上第一读者呢！

我眼中的 ⌢……

好书，爱不释手！

★ 读者 王汐子（女，2009年留学美国，攻读大学传媒专业）《小屁孩日记》在美国掀起的阅读风潮可不是盖的，在我留学美国的这一年中，不止一次目睹这套书对太平洋彼岸人民的巨大影响。高速公路上巨大的广告宣传牌就不用说了，我甚至在学校书店买课本时看到了这套书被大大咧咧地摆上书架，"小屁孩"的搞笑日记就这样理直气壮地充当起了美国大学生的课本教材！为什么这套书如此受欢迎？为什么一个普普通通的小男孩能让这么多成年人捧腹大笑？也许可以套用一个万能句式"每个人心中都有一个XXX"。每个人心中都有一个小屁孩，每个人小时候也有过这样的时光，每天都有点鸡毛蒜皮的小烦恼，像作业这么多怎么办啦，要考试了书都没有看怎么办啦……但是大部分时候还是因为调皮捣蛋被妈妈教训……就这样迷迷糊糊地走过了"小屁孩"时光，等长大后和朋友们讨论后才恍然大悟，随即不禁感慨，原来那时候我们都一样呀……是呀，全世界的小屁孩都一样！

★ 读者 zhizhimother（发表于2009-06-12）在杂志上看到这书的介绍，一时冲动在当当上下了单，没想到，一买回来一家人抢着看，笑得前仰后合。我跟女儿一人抢到一本，老公很不满意，他嘟囔着下一本出的时候他要第一个看。看多了面孔雷同的好孩子的书，看到这本，真是深有感触，我们的孩子其实都是这样长大的！

轻松阅读　捧腹大笑

★　这是著名的畅销书作家小巫的儿子Sam口述的英语和中文读后感：我喜欢《小屁孩日记》，因为Greg是跟我们一样的普通孩子。他的故事很好玩儿，令我捧腹大笑，他做的事情很搞笑，有点儿傻乎乎的。书里的插图也很幽默。

★　读者 dearm暖baby（发表于2009-07-29）我12岁了，过生日时妈妈给我买了这样两本书，真的很有趣！一半是中文，一半是英文，彻底打破了"英文看不懂看下面中文"的局限！而且这本书彻底地给我来了次大放松，"重点中学"的压力也一扫而光！总之，两个字：超赞！

孩子爱上写日记了！

★　读者 ddian2003（发表于2009-12-22）正是于丹的那几句话吸引我买下了这套书。自己倒没看，但女儿却用了三天学校的课余时间就看完了，随后她大受启发，连着几天都写了日记。现在这书暂时搁在书柜里，已和女儿约定，等她学了英文后再来看一遍，当然要看书里的英文了。所以这书还是买得物有所值的。毕竟女儿喜欢！！

做个"不听话的好孩子"

★　读者 水真爽（发表于2010-03-27）这套书是买给我上小学二年级的儿子的。有时候他因为到该读书的时间而被要求从网游下来很恼火。尽管带着气，甚至眼泪，可是读起这本书来，总是能被书中小屁孩的种种淘气出格行为和想法弄得哈哈大笑。书中的卡通漫画也非常不错。这种文字漫画形式的日记非常具有趣味性，老少咸宜。对低年级孩子或爱画漫画的孩子尤其有启发作用。更重要的是提醒家长们要好好留意观察这些"不怎么听话"的小屁孩们的内心世界，他们的健康成长需要成人的呵护引导，但千万不要把他们都变成只会"听大人话"的好孩子。

对照《小屁孩日记》分享育儿体验

★ 读者 gjrzj2002@＊＊＊.＊＊＊（发表于2010-05-21）看完四册书，我想着自己虽然不可能有三个孩子，但一个孩子的成长经历至今仍记忆犹新。儿子还是幼儿的时候，比较像曼尼，在爸妈眼中少有缺点，真是让人越看越爱，想要什么就基本上能得到什么。整个幼儿期父母对孩子肯定大过否定。上了小学，儿子的境地就不怎么从容了，上学的压力时时处处在影响着他，小家伙要承受各方面的压力，父母、老师、同学，太过我行我素、大而化之都是行不通的，比如没写作业的话，老师、家长的批评和提醒是少不了的，孩子在慢慢学着适应这种生活，烦恼也随之而来，这一阶段比较像格雷，虽然儿子的思维还没那么丰富，快乐和烦恼的花样都没那么多，但处境差不多，表扬和赞美不像以前那样轻易就能得到了。儿子青年时代会是什么样子我还不得而知，也不可想象，那种水到渠成的阶段要靠前面的积累，我希望自己到时候能平心静气，坦然接受，无论儿子成长成什么样子。

气味相投的好伙伴

★ 上海市外国语大学附属第一实验中学，中预10班，沈昕仪Elaine：《小屁孩日记》读来十分轻松。虽然没有用十分华丽的语言，却使我感受到了小屁孩那缤纷多彩的生活，给我带来无限的欢乐。那精彩的插图、幽默的文字实在是太有趣了，当中的故事在我们身边都有可能发生，让人身临其境。格雷总能说出我的心里话，他是和我有着共同语言的朋友。所以他们搞的恶作剧一直让我跃跃欲试，也想找一次机会尝试一下。不知道别的读者怎么想，我觉得格雷挺喜欢出风头的。我也是这样的人，总怕别人无视自己。当看到格雷蹦出那些稀奇古怪的点子的时候，我多想帮他一把啊——毕竟我们是"气味相投"的同类人嘛。另一方面，我身处在外语学校，时刻都需要积累英语单词，但这件事总是让我觉得枯燥乏味。而《小屁孩日记》帮了我的大忙：我在享受快乐阅读的同时，还可以对照中英文学到很多常用英语单词。我发现其实生活中还有很多事情值得我们去用笔写下来。即使是小事，这些童年的故事也是很值得我们回忆的。既然还生活在童年，还能够写下那些故事，又何乐而不为呢？

画出我心中的"小屁孩"

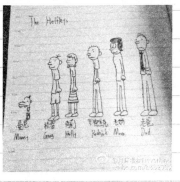

邓博笔下的赫夫利一家

读者@童_Cc.与@曲奇做的"小屁孩"手抄报

亲爱的读者，你看完这本书后，有什么感想吗？请来电或是登录本书的博客与我们分享吧！等本书再版时，这里也许换上了你的读后感呢！

我们的电话号码是：020-83795744；博客地址是：blog.sina.com.cn/wimpykid；微博地址是：weibo.com/wimpywimpy。